THE HIDDEN WORLD OF

Changers

No. 6: The Spirit Warrior

by H. K. Varian

Simon Spotlight
New York London Toronto Sydney New Delhi

This book is a work of fiction. Any references to historical events, real people, or real places are used fictitiously. Other names, characters, places, and events are products of the author's imagination, and any resemblance to actual events or places or persons, living or dead, is entirely coincidental.

SIMON SPOTLIGHT
An imprint of Simon & Schuster Children's Publishing Division
1230 Avenue of the Americas, New York, New York 10020
This Simon Spotlight edition March 2017

Text by Laurie Calkhoven
Illustrations by Tony Foti

Designed by Nick Sciacca
The text of this book was set in Celestia Antiqua.
Manufactured in the United States of America 0217 FFG
10 9 8 7 6 5 4 3 2 1
ISBN 978-1-4814-8085-7 (hc)
ISBN 978-1-4814-8084-0 (pbk)
ISBN 978-1-4814-8086-4 (eBook)
Library of Congress Catalog Card Number 2016939210

Nahual

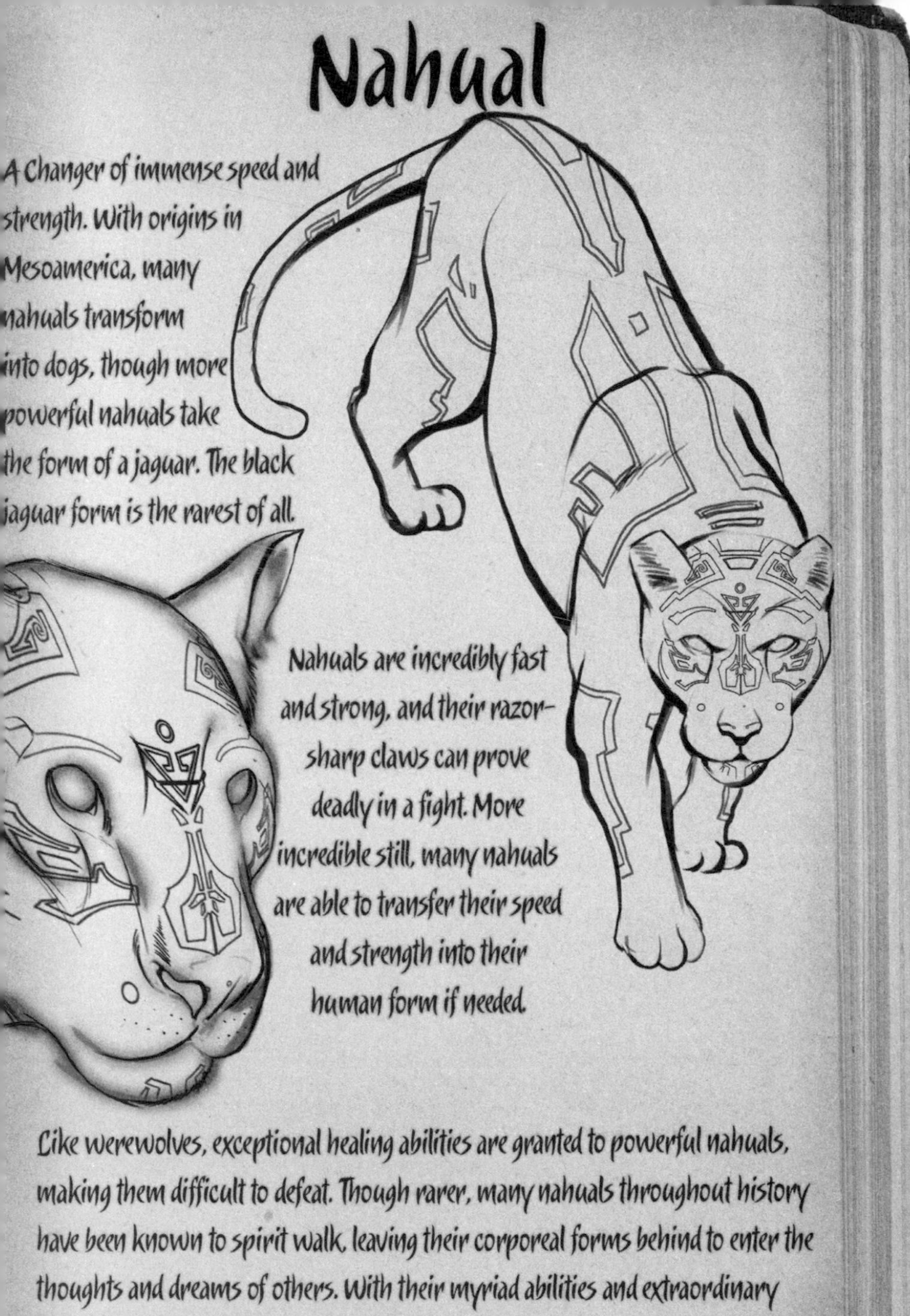

A Changer of immense speed and strength. With origins in Mesoamerica, many nahuals transform into dogs, though more powerful nahuals take the form of a jaguar. The black jaguar form is the rarest of all.

Nahuals are incredibly fast and strong, and their razor-sharp claws can prove deadly in a fight. More incredible still, many nahuals are able to transfer their speed and strength into their human form if needed.

Like werewolves, exceptional healing abilities are granted to powerful nahuals, making them difficult to defeat. Though rarer, many nahuals throughout history have been known to spirit walk, leaving their corporeal forms behind to enter the thoughts and dreams of others. With their myriad abilities and extraordinary fighting prowess, the nahual is not a Changer to anger.

PROLOGUE

Gabriella Rivera rushed out of math class the second the bell rang. She needed to talk to her friends Fiona Murphy and Darren Smith before their next and final class of the day. It was a class that the rest of Willow Cove Middle School *thought* was an ordinary gym class, but Gabriella and her friends knew that it was so much more.

Gabriella zigzagged around clusters of other kids, making her way back to her locker. Sometimes, in the midst of her fellow students, it was easy to forget just how different she was from them—just how different everything was. Gabriella had learned on the first day of seventh grade that she was a Changer, someone with the power to transform into a creature the normal world believed was mythological.

In Gabriella's case, she had discovered she was a *nahual*, or jaguar, from Aztec mythology. Her aunt and grandmother had always been proud of their Mexican heritage, and they always insisted that the blood of Aztec warriors ran through their veins, but until recently, Gabriella had no idea how true that family story actually was. With her transformation came an array of incredible powers worthy of any warrior—superspeed, sharp claws, and quick reflexes, among other things.

Gabriella caught up with Fiona and Darren near Fiona's locker. Fiona was the secret daughter of the *selkie* queen, a seal Changer who ruled the oceans. Using her *selkie* cloak, Fiona could transform into a seal as well; in her human form she channeled magic into *selkie* songs. Darren's other form was a fearsome bird, an *impundulu*, who could shoot lightning bolts from his razor-sharp talons and create incredible storms. The final member of their group was Makoto "Mack" Kimura.

"Have you seen Mack yet?" Gabriella asked.

Darren shook his head.

"He wasn't in homeroom," Fiona murmured, glancing around to make sure she wouldn't be overheard. "When I called his house last night, his grandfather said Mack would be here for Changers class. The First Four will be here too, so Mack could transform for the first time since . . ." Her voice trailed off.

"Since Sakura bit him," Gabriella said bluntly.

Mack, a huge fan of comic books and superheroes, could transform into a *kitsune*, a magical fox whose paws blazed with fire. Mack could be goofy and more than a bit nerdy at times, but Gabriella liked that he always saw the best in people. When each of his friends, including Gabriella, had trouble controlling their powers, Mack never lost faith in them. He was always the first to say that things were going to work out okay.

Mack's grandfather, Akira Kimura, was also a *kitsune* and one of the First Four—a council of elders who led Changers all over the world. But even Mack's powerful grandfather couldn't protect him from the Changers' newest enemy, an evil *kitsune* named Sakura, known to many as the Shadow Fox.

Kitsune earn tails (up to nine) for accomplishing heroic deeds or learning new skills. One of Sakura's unique abilities was memory eating, which meant that she could consume other Changers' memories and, in doing so, could also absorb their powers. A former student of Mr. Kimura's, she had delved into dark magic and when that went very, very wrong, Sakura turned on Mr. Kimura. She even started a rebellion against the First Four, and stole powers from many Changers. Her exploits had made her a boogeyman to most younglings. Sakura had since been hiding from the Changers, watching and waiting for her chance to strike. But recently, she had returned and pledged to stop at nothing to have her revenge on Mr. Kimura and the rest of the First Four. That included going after Mr. Kimura's grandson, Mack.

Gabriella and the other young Changers—or younglings, as the Changer world called them—had been back in Willow Cove for only a few days. Over their school's spring break, they had visited Wyndemere Academy, a boarding school for high school–aged Changers. Mack and his friends were supposed to get to know the school and participate in a competition known as the Youngling Games. But Sakura had put a stop to all that, bringing fear and chaos to the Changer world once again.

Sakura had been following Mack for some time, but Mack's grandfather refused to talk to him about her. Frustrated with his grandfather, and determined to get his own answers, Mack followed Sakura and confronted her. Unfortunately, he did so without knowing just how dangerous she could be.

Fiona had saved Mack's life with a *selkie* song—arguably one of the most powerful forms of magic known to Changers—but not before Sakura managed to sink her teeth into their friend. Mack had been unable to tell them what happened and what memories or powers Sakura had stolen from him, but he did know one thing: War was coming. War between Sakura's followers and those who supported the First Four. The First Four were dedicated to protecting humans and Changers alike. Sakura wanted to take the world for Changer-kind alone.

Gabriella shivered thinking about the dark times

ahead. Her mother and sister were normal, nonmagical people; so were her soccer teammates and most of her friends. She would do whatever she could to protect them. She hoped to learn more about how to do that and how to defeat Sakura in today's class. And, of course, she also hoped to see Mack.

"Do you think he'll be okay?" Darren asked. "I mean, what if Sakura took his power—like, *stole* it?"

"Mack's our friend, powers or not," Gabriella said. "It's important that we're there for him."

"I wish Mr. Kimura would have let us visit Mack over the weekend," Fiona said. "He was so upset when we saw him last. . . . I'm afraid Mack will think we abandoned him."

"Mack knows we've got his back," Darren said. "The four of us need one another. We're not complete without him. Now let's go so we can tell him that in person."

"There's Mack," Gabriella said as they entered the school's ancillary gym.

Mack and his grandfather were standing in a corner, having a discussion in Japanese. Mr. Kimura had a hand on his grandson's shoulder, as if he was trying to reassure him. Gabriella saw Mack's eyes flick in their direction for a second before he turned his attention back to his grandfather.

He looks different, Gabriella thought. *Guarded.*

Dorina Therian, their primary coach and another member of the First Four, greeted Gabriella and the others. She was the one who had given Gabriella the news that she was a *nahual* the first day of class and then demonstrated her own Changer transformation—into a werewolf.

The other two members of the First Four, Sefu Badawi (a *bultungin*, or hyena Changer) and Yara Moreno (an *encantado*, or dolphin Changer) also waited. They smiled reassuringly at Gabriella and her friends.

Mack and his grandfather finished their conversation and joined the group.

"Ready to get this over with?" Mack asked with a queasy smile. "Let's make sure I haven't sprouted a new head or grown an extra row of teeth or . . . lost my powers."

"It's going to be fine," Fiona said. "*You're* going to be fine."

"Of course you are," Gabriella added, giving him a quick hug.

"Yeah, we're here for you no matter what," Darren said.

Mack's queasy smile returned, but he said nothing.

They waited for the First Four to clue them in on what was about to happen.

"I don't want any of you to be frightened," Mr. Kimura said. "Chances are that this is all for nothing, and Makoto will be able to transform without issue. It's important we're together though."

While he was speaking, the other members of the First Four formed a kind of square around Mack. Ms. Therian motioned for Gabriella, Darren, and Fiona to stand a bit farther back, filling in the gaps between their elders.

"Darren, if you would, a force field around all of us for protection might be helpful," Mr. Kimura said.

Darren nodded. Soon, the tips of his fingers were crackling with electricity, forming sparks. While Gabriella watched, those sparks joined together, creating a glowing web. Moments later, the force field encircled all eight of them.

Why would we need a force field if this is just about Mack transforming? Gabriella wondered. *Is Mr. Kimura keeping others out of the circle or making sure Mack can't escape?*

"I'm going to count down, Makoto," Mr. Kimura said. "When I reach one, you can transform."

Mack nodded, his expression grim.

Gabriella's shoulders tightened as Mr. Kimura began to count from ten to one. Even without thinking she was on the balls of her feet, ready to spring into action if needed.

But I won't need to, she thought. *This is only about Mack's transformation.*

Still, she felt her own tension increase with each second. She couldn't imagine what Mack was thinking and feeling. She stared into his face, but his eyes were clouded. With worry? Fear? Anger? She couldn't tell.

"Three, two, one," Mr. Kimura said. He nodded at his grandson.

Gabriella held her breath. Mack transformed, just like she had seen him do so many times before, and he was . . .

Mack! The same as always.

Gabriella exhaled when she saw that her friend had transformed into a fox with sandy-red fur—just like he always had. Orange and yellow flames licked at his paws. Gabriella smiled at him, and Mack seemed to smile back. But then she saw confusion on the faces of Ms. Therian, Fiona, and Sefu, who were standing behind him.

Mack looked over his shoulder, and when he did, Gabriella saw the cause of their confusion.

Mack had gained a third tail.

Chapter 1
THE THIRD TAIL

Mack spun around to look at his new tail. I—I *don't remember earning it*, Mack thought. He looked to his grandfather for an explanation. *Jiichan?*

The memory of when Mack had earned his second tail came flooding back to him: It was right after his battle with the evil warlock, Auden Ironbound. He'd saved his grandfather and his friends. He was sure he'd never forget that burst of self-confidence and pride. But Mack didn't feel proud now. All he felt was panic.

His grandfather and the rest of the First Four exchanged glances. "Transform back, Makoto, and we'll talk," his grandfather said.

When he did, the First Four visibly relaxed from their previous ready-for-battle positions. Ms. Therian motioned for Darren to release the force field.

A sudden angry thought burst into Mack's mind. *Was that force field because they were afraid they'd have to fight me?* He stayed in the middle of the circle, waiting for someone to say something, his temper flaring again. *Why isn't anyone talking?*

Fiona stepped forward and finally broke the silence. "Isn't this a good thing?" she asked. "Mack must have done something heroic to earn another tail, right? And maybe Sakura ate that memory, which explains why he doesn't remember."

Mack felt a little better hearing Fiona's words, but his grandfather's eyes still held that worried expression.

"It must have been something really powerful," Fiona said more forcefully. "Powerful enough that Sakura had to destroy the memory so Mack wouldn't remember how to do it again."

Mack wanted more than anything to believe her, but then he saw Jiichan catch Ms. Therian's eye.

Mack's panic turned to irritation. *They're having a telepathic conversation about me,* he thought. *Jiichan promised to stop keeping so many secrets, and now here's another one.* No *wonder Sakura—*

Mack shook his head to stop the thought. Jiichan kept telling him not to think too much about her. She might have planted ugly, false beliefs in his mind.

Before anyone else noticed what was going on between his grandfather and his teacher, Yara told everyone to take a seat. They all headed over to the bench.

"Before we left for Wyndemere Academy, we told you of the prophecy that the four of you are destined to become the next leaders of the Changer nation. When we, the current First Four, step down, you'll step up to take on our mantle," Yara said.

"That's a long way off, though, right?" Fiona asked. "Changers live for a thousand years or more."

Yara smiled, her face a wreath of wrinkles. "Yes, a way off, but there will come a time when our leadership will end. You need to be ready when that time comes."

"We hoped to wait until you were fully trained, until after you had a chance to go to Wyndemere Academy for high school to begin this process. Given recent events, however, we want you to be more fully aware,"

Ms. Therian said. "That's why we promised to keep you informed and involved in Changer affairs. No more secrets."

Mack snorted to himself. *You and Jiichan were just telling secrets—about me!*

Ms. Therian continued. "With Sakura back, we're going to have to make some preparations—"

"You mean prepare for war," Mack cut in.

There was an awkward pause.

"Prepare for war," Sefu repeated with a nod. "Sakura's forces have made themselves known. There were skirmishes over the weekend. We have enchantments to keep them at bay, for now, but they're already nipping at our heels. The special attention we've given the four of you might have tipped them off to the prophecy. That makes you high-value targets."

"And we already know that Sakura wants to use Mack to hurt his grandfather," Ms. Therian added. "The four of you must be on guard, ready to fight at all times."

"Are her forces under some sort of mind control like Auden Ironbound's were? Did she eat their memories to turn them against us?" Fiona asked.

There was silence for a moment while the First Four pondered how to answer Fiona's question.

Mack remembered battling—and defeating—Auden Ironbound on the beach in Willow Cove. At least Sakura hadn't stolen *that* memory. The evil warlock had used the Horn of Power to force Changers to follow him. Adult Changers were unable to resist his call and were poised to help him take over the world. But the horn didn't affect younglings. With the help of his Changer friends, Mack had won their first battle against Auden and saved the First Four.

Did Jiichan and Ms. Therian remember that when they were having their secret conversation? he wondered. *That I saved them from Auden?*

"That's a very good question, Fiona," Sefu said. "But that's not the case. Sakura has to exert a tremendous amount of power for memory eating. It can leave her feeling weak and vulnerable afterward. That may be why you were able to drive her away from Mack with the Queen's Song, just like you were able to defeat Auden."

Wow, Fiona gets the credit? Mack thought. Fiona was

the one who ultimately defeated Auden and destroyed the horn, but Mack thought *his* battle with the warlock had been much more difficult than Fiona's. And Sefu didn't even bother to mention it.

Mack shook his head again. *What's wrong with me? This isn't a competition. Fiona is my friend.*

"What about absorbing other Changers' powers?" Darren asked. "I mean, couldn't she just take all her followers' powers and become really strong?"

"True, but the best strength is in numbers," Sefu continued. "She would need an army to take out all of our forces and overturn the world order. She needs people around her who have their powers intact."

"So the people who have joined her have done so because they want to?" Darren asked.

Sefu nodded. "I'm afraid so."

"But why would anyone turn against the Changer nation?" Gabriella asked. "It doesn't make sense."

Mack felt the wisp of a memory tickling the back of his mind. At the sound of Mack taking a deep breath, everyone turned to him.

"I feel like—like I remember something Sakura

said. It was about being free," he added. "Like how the *selkies* split—"

Mr. Kimura cut Mack off before he could finish. "It's best that you don't try to remember your encounter with Sakura. Your memories might be corrupted, replaced with what Sakura *wants* you to remember."

Mack pressed his lips together to keep angry words from escaping. I *was only trying to help*, he thought.

Sefu smiled at Mack reassuringly before continuing. "The Changer nation provides Changers with support in navigating their daily lives, keeping our powers secret, and building families and communities. But we also have a more central goal of protecting nonmagical people. That's something the Changers have been doing since the dawn of time."

"Sakura doesn't share that sense of purpose," Ms. Therian added. "She'd rather see nonmagical beings turned into slaves or eliminated completely."

"So her followers want the same thing?" Gabriella asked.

"Some do," Ms. Therian answered. "Others have different reasons. There are Changers who dislike having to go on periodic missions as part of their service to the nation. Still more don't like the way we track the whereabouts of all magical beings, or they believe the First Four are too powerful. We try hard not to overstep our boundaries, but sometimes we have to put these precautions in place to ensure the future of all people, magical or not."

"Without the power the First Four hold, ordinary humans would be at much greater risk from magical threats," Yara added. "Without regular service from Changers, magical relics could fall into evil hands, and without the ability to track Changers and other magical beings, it would be easier to commit magical crimes."

"That all makes sense," Darren said, "if you only use your power to do good."

"I agree," Yara said. "I think this power is necessary, but others don't feel the same. When the four of you become the next First Four, you will have to tackle these same issues."

Mack's grandfather had been quiet, but now he passed out folders with information to each of them.

"To battle Sakura and her army, we need to retrieve certain enchanted objects that protect against mind control. Without them, you'll be vulnerable to Sakura's powers; it's very important that you take the necessary steps to defend yourselves."

Are you kidding? Mack thought. *There was an enchanted object that might have protected me from Sakura, and you're only telling me this now?*

"Why don't we already have them?" Mack asked out loud. He tried to keep the sarcastic edge out of his voice, but it colored his tone, anyway. "Since we're targets?"

"Many of these objects are hidden away," his grandfather answered. "Deeply hidden. Our mission is to find them."

He turned to Gabriella. "I want you to have the Ring of Tezcatlipoca," he said, handing it to her.

Mack remembered that Gabriella had used the ring to help fight Auden Ironbound's followers during their final battle. It only worked for those from an Aztec bloodline, like Gabriella.

Gabriella slipped the ring onto her finger. There was

a soft crackling sound, and the air around her seemed to shimmer for a moment, as though she was surrounded by some invisible force field. The ring was made of pure gold and obsidian with an elaborate carving of a man's face on the front, and beautiful designs along the band. A horizontal streak of black ran across the center of the man's face. More importantly, the ancient artifact gave its wearer the spiritual strength to resist mind control magic.

"Keep it on at all times, Gabriella," Mr. Kimura added. "I've cast a cloaking spell on it, so no one should notice you're wearing it. Whatever you do, do not lose the ring."

Gabriella twisted the golden ring nervously. "I'll be careful," she said.

"And, Fiona," Mr. Kimura said, "the knowledge of the Queen's Song is also a protection. The two of you won't fall prey to Sakura's memory eating."

Mack and Darren exchanged uneasy glances. I *guess we're out of luck*, Mack thought.

It was as if his grandfather heard him. "Over the next weeks we'll be searching for enchanted objects—some of them hidden away for centuries—that will protect Mack and Darren. It's urgent that we find them before Sakura does."

"Saturday night is our first mission. We'll be traveling to Japan the same way we went to Wyndemere—with a *tengu* Changer," Ms. Therian said as the bell rang. "Read over the mission brief tonight and bring your questions to class tomorrow."

Japan! Mack felt hopeful for the first time since he got back from Wyndemere Academy. He had never been there, but it was his grandfather and his parents' birthplace. For a long time, Mack had tried to push away his Japanese heritage and the traditions that his grandfather cherished.

But ever since Mack had learned that he was a *kitsune*, a Changer so rooted in Japanese folklore, he'd felt a longing to go there that he hadn't yet put into words. Things between his grandfather and himself had been a bit off since he first saw Sakura after the battle with Auden, and the tension was only getting worse. There was a part of Mack that wanted to lean on his grandfather after what had happened, and another part that wanted to push everyone away and be alone. In the last few days, Mack had felt at war with himself.

Maybe I'll find the protection I need in Japan, Mack thought. *Willow Cove doesn't feel safe anymore.*

Chapter 2
The Secret Mission

Gabriella shoved the folder about their mission into her backpack and got up leave with the others. Then she received a telepathic message from Ms. Therian.

Hang on, Gabriella, Ms. Therian communicated. *The First Four need to speak with you about something.*

Gabriella smiled and waved as Fiona and Darren disappeared past the double doors. Once she was sure they were gone, she turned to Ms. Therian. "What's going on?" she asked.

"We have a special mission we'd like to propose," Ms. Therian said. "But it's rather risky."

"It's entirely within your rights to refuse if you're not ready," Sefu added.

Not ready? Not ready for what? Gabriella thought.

Mack was still sitting in the middle of the First Four, staring at the floor. He didn't look up to meet Gabriella's eyes.

"What kind of mission?" she asked.

"Makoto might not be the same after his encounter with Sakura," Yara admitted. "It's possible that she altered some of his memories or even planted false ones in his mind. The tail he earned, while it's true that he might have done something brave . . ." Her voice trailed off.

"She could have gifted him with a dark ability," Sefu finished bluntly. "Sakura can steal other Changers' powers, but she can also transfer those powers to her victims as well. It's one of her unique abilities, like memory eating, that she gained through dark magic."

"Sakura would never willingly give up her prey the way she did with Mack," Ms. Therian said. "We suspect she did that for a reason. She could be planning to use him as a pawn in the coming war. It's even possible that Mack is unknowingly feeding her information about us."

Mack still didn't raise his head. Gabriella's heart ached for him, for how frightened he must be. *Poor Mack . . . After everything that happened at Wyndemere, you'd think he's been through enough. And now this?*

"I thought it was Fiona's song that drove the Shadow Fox away," Gabriella said. "That if Sakura stayed, her powers would have been destroyed, like Auden Ironbound's."

"We hope that is the case," Ms. Therian said gently. "But she may have left Mack behind on purpose. We don't know enough yet about Sakura's plans. It's more likely that she has a bigger role in mind for Mack, one that might already be set in motion. There's no sure way for us to tell—"

Yara interrupted. "There is something that might provide the answers we need: spirit-walking. If you're willing."

Spirit-walking? But that's superdangerous. The last time I did it, it was only because no other nahuals *were around.*

Spirit-walking was a skill that only very powerful *nahuals* could master. They could enter the dreams and thoughts of others, but it was highly dangerous. Untrained *nahuals* could also lose themselves in the process, if their spirits couldn't find their way back to their bodies.

Gabriella could feel a whisper of panic start in her heart and then spread through her. She wasn't ready for such a mission. She remembered spirit-walking into Darren's mind when he was being held captive by Auden Ironbound's forces. She had only just managed to make it back.

"I only spirit-walked once, and that was a huge emergency," she said.

"It is your right to refuse," Mr. Kimura reminded her.

"It's not that," Gabriella began, looking to Mack sympathetically. "I want to do it more than anything, but I just . . . don't think I'm ready. You should ask my Tía Rosa or my grandmother or another *nahual*," Gabriella added. "I could fail, and this is too important."

There was a long pause.

"We're very proud of you, Gabriella," Mrs. Therian said earnestly.

"'Proud'?" Gabriella echoed.

Her teacher nodded. "A few months ago you would have rushed headlong into this mission without knowing all the dangers. But you've grown. You've learned that there's more at risk here than your own safety. That having been said, we have the utmost confidence in you—not just that you can do this, but that you're the only one who can."

"Do you remember what Mr. Kimura said when we told you about the prophecy? About the bond that the First Four share?" Yara asked.

Gabriella nodded.

"Do you remember how you and Fiona and Mack could sense Darren's pain and fear when he was kidnapped by Auden Ironbound's forces? And also when Darren unleashed his powers?"

"I remember," Gabriella said. She and the others had been so scared for Darren, and equally determined to save him.

"The four of you—the next First Four—share a powerful bond. That bond could alert you to anything in Mack's mind that is out of place, that doesn't belong. Another *nahual* wouldn't be as attuned," Ms. Therian said. "If we're to discover what Sakura did to Mack, you're our best hope—and Mack's too."

Gabriella thought about that for a minute, her eyes on Mack. *Does he want me to do this?* she wondered. *How does he feel about the idea of me wandering through his thoughts?*

As if he knew what she was thinking, Mack finally raised his head.

"If someone's going to be walking around in my brain, I'd rather it was you than some total stranger," he said. Then he gave her a kind of twisted smile. "But you have to promise not to steal any of my comic book ideas, because I'm planning on making it big with the new superhero I've come up with."

Gabriella smiled back. It was good to hear Mack sound like Mack again, if only for a minute. Her panic subsided a little bit. She started to think that maybe she could try.

"You're going to need a lot of training—and fast—if you're willing to take on this mission," Mr. Kimura said. "Most *nahuals* spend years learning to master this ability, but you only have weeks."

"Weeks?" Gabriella sputtered. "Why? What do you think will happen?"

"It's vital that we discover Sakura's plan and ensure Mack's safety as soon as possible. It will take a fierce dedication, but I know you have it in you to succeed."

Maybe I *do have it in me*, she thought. *If* I *work really hard to learn what* I *need to*, I *can help Mack.*

Suddenly, the gym doors burst open. Tía Rosa and Gabriella's grandmother, whom she called Abuelita, entered the room. Although Gabriella's mother and sister knew nothing about her secret Changer world, Gabriella had inherited her Changer ability from her grandmother, and her aunt had too.

It had been a huge relief to turn to them for help in the early, confusing days when she could barely control her powers and was constantly afraid she'd transform at the wrong place and time. For a while, she had been just one unintentional transformation away from exposing her secret self to the world, until Tía Rosa stepped in. For a few months now, Rosa had been training Gabriella to control her transformations and master her fighting skills.

"Sorry we're late," Tía Rosa said with a wave. "This one"—she nudged Abuelita—"insisted on lunching at the Willow Cove Café, even though the line was out the door."

Abuelita rolled her eyes and shrugged. "They have good burgers. Do you know how often I get to eat a good burger at my age?"

"Tía Rosa! Abuelita!" Gabriella said as her aunt embraced her. "What are you doing here?"

Abuelita tottered over and placed her hands on Gabriella's cheeks. "If you decide to take on this mission, we've agreed to handle your training."

Gabriella looked from her grandmother to her aunt and back again.

I don't want to disappoint them—especially Mack, she thought to them. *But do you think I can really do this?*

Tía Rosa put an arm around her niece. *Mija, I'm surprised at you! Our Gabriella, hesitant to take on a challenge? It's true, you'll be facing the same risks you faced when you entered Darren's mind, and entering Mack's mind will have added dangers. We don't know exactly what Sakura did to him.*

But . . . you think I can do it? Gabriella asked again.

Tía Rosa nodded. *I have no doubt. You're strong—much stronger than either of us were at your age. I've seen you overcome so many obstacles in such a short amount of time. You're going to be just fine.*

We'll do everything in our power to make sure you succeed, her grandmother added. *And come back to us safely.*

Gabriella felt her determination growing. Tía Rosa was right. Gabriella had never before been afraid to take on a challenge or to do what was right, no matter the odds. She'd trained with her aunt in combat and had gotten so good that she fended off an army of Changers with nothing but her claws—*twice*. It was time to shake off her fears and do whatever she could to save her friend.

She turned to the group, who was waiting patiently for her answer. "I'll do my best," she said with a wave of renewed confidence. "I'll start training right now."

Mr. Kimura bowed to her. "We owe you our gratitude."

Gabriella caught Mack's eye and nodded. He nodded back.

"Mack would do it for me," she said.

"I must ask you to keep this mission a secret from Fiona and Darren for now. The fewer people who know what we're about to try, the better," Mr. Kimura said.

"I won't tell anyone," Gabriella promised. Then she turned to her family. "So . . . when do we start?"

Later that night, Gabriella, Abuelita, and Tía Rosa sat around the dinner table with Gabriella's younger sister, Maritza, and their mother.

Abuelita and Tía Rosa, who stayed after school to watch Gabriella's track practice, made jokes about getting tickets for the upcoming Olympics. They wanted to be sure they had good seats when Gabriella won her gold medals.

It seemed like a regular family dinner, but all the while, Gabriella couldn't feel entirely at ease. Thinking about the special training she would have to undergo was making her impatient to get started. She was thinking about that when Abuelita changed the topic of conversation.

"You know what?" Abuelita said, looking around the table. "I don't spend enough time like this with the four of you. I know I was only going to visit for a few days, but I think I'll stay longer."

She put one hand on Gabriella's shoulder and the other on Maritza's. "I need a vacation from my retirement, and I can't think of a better way to spend my time than with my favorite daughters and granddaughters."

"We're your *only* daughters, Ma," Gabriella's mother said with a smile.

"And your *only* granddaughters," Maritza added.

"Yes, I know that, and you're all my favorites," Abuelita said with a laugh. She turned to Gabriella and added, "What do you think, *mija*? Can you put up with me for a month?"

"Of course I can," Gabriella said, giving her a hug.

Tía Rosa chimed in. "I have some vacation time coming, too," she said. Rosa lived close by in New Brighton, the nearest city to Willow Cove. "Do you mind having a full house for a couple of weeks, Isabel?"

Gabriella's mom laughed. "Only if you promise not to leave the house a pigsty like you usually do!"

The whole family burst into laughter. Gabriella knew that her *abuelita* and *tía* would really be sticking around for her training, but Ma and Maritza were just happy to have them around. For a few hours, Gabriella tried her best to push aside her worries about Mack and spirit-walking and Sakura and enjoy being a normal kid with her family. The next steps would come soon enough.

Abuelita tucked Maritza into bed a couple of hours later and then made her way to Gabriella's bedroom.

"I'm too old to be tucked in," Gabriella said with a sleepy smile.

"Never!" her grandmother scoffed. She sat on the side of the bed and tucked Gabriella's blanket around her. "Sleep tight. Tomorrow's going to be a big day—your first day of training. And don't expect us to go easy on you."

"I won't," Gabriella said. "I have to be ready to help Mack."

"You will be," Abuelita promised, turning out the light.

She had smiled when she'd said it, but that didn't mask the worry Gabriella had seen in her grandmother's eyes. She felt a mix of emotions as Abuelita left the room and closed the door behind her. It was going to be really cool to spend more time with her *nahual* family members and to learn more about spirit-walking. But there was a lot of pressure too. What if she failed?

Because after all, didn't the First Four say that if I can't save Mack from the Shadow Fox, no one can?

Chapter 3
THE TIDE SONG

Fiona yawned and stretched before getting out of bed the next morning. Her dreams were filled with worries about Mack, and she was anxious to get to school to see him. She quickly ran through her morning routine, checked her homework, and was getting dressed when she smelled something wonderful wafting up from the kitchen—pancakes!

"Dad, I thought you were leaving early for the poetry conference!" she said, padding down the stairs. "Did your presentation get cancelled?" She rounded the corner into the kitchen to find not her father but her *mother* in front of the stove, wielding the pancake ladle.

For most kids, the scene before her would feel completely normal. But until recently, Fiona had thought that her mother passed away when she was still a toddler. About ten years ago, there was a rift between the *selkies* and the Changer nation. Her mother, as queen of *selkies*, had left Fiona and her nonmagical father to lead the *selkies* and prevent all-out war between the two factions. Ever since, there had been an uneasy peace between the *selkies* and the rest of the Changers. Fiona's father told her that her mother had died, and Fiona only learned the truth after she discovered she was a Changer herself and would be the next *selkie* queen.

Ever since they reconnected, Fiona had cherished the moments she spent with her mother. Their meetings had always taken place in the ocean waters or on the *selkie*-controlled Isles of Saorsie, where Mom would teach her daughter the *selkie* ways and their magical songs. Fiona hadn't seen her mother in the cottage she shared with her father since she was three.

And now she was right here in the kitchen making pancakes!

"Mom! You're here," Fiona said.

Mom pulled Fiona into a hug. "I wanted to see you, so I thought I'd come by for breakfast. Chocolate chip pancakes used to be your favorite. Are they still?"

"They are," Fiona said. "You remembered!"

"I remember everything about you," Mom said with a smile.

"And I remember the smell of coffee brewing in the morning while you made the pancakes," Fiona added, eyeing the empty coffeemaker. "Have you given it up?"

Mom laughed. "I can't figure it out!" she said. "Technology has certainly changed in the past ten years. It looks more like a spaceship than a coffeepot. Can you help?"

"When I'm the first one up, I make Dad's coffee. I'll make yours too."

Soon, the two of them were settled down to a breakfast of fresh fruit, pancakes, and two cups of coffee for Mom. Fiona wished that all her mornings could be this wonderful. It just needed one more thing to make it perfect: Dad. Someday she hoped the fragile peace between the *selkies* and the rest of the Changers would grow into a real alliance and they could all live together again.

As long as distrust continued between the Changers and her own subjects, Mom felt that she had to remain where she was—in the ocean with the *selkie* faction. Fiona knew that her mother longed to bring the two groups together again—with Fiona's help. Fiona wanted the same thing, so that the two of them could spend a lot more time together. For now, she had to settle for weekend *selkie* lessons and occasional surprise visits.

"Have you been practicing the new song I taught you?" Mom asked.

Fiona held up one finger and sang a few notes. A glowing wave symbol appeared on her palm, and then there was a loud whooshing sound. Her mother looked out the window to see a huge wave crash on the rocky shore—a wave Fiona had summoned.

"Amazing!" Mom said. "At this rate you'll have most of the songs mastered before you even come of age."

Fiona smiled. *It feels so good to hear love and pride in my mother's voice when she talks about me.*

"With everything that's been going on, I want to learn them fast. I feel better knowing I can defend myself on land if I have to," Fiona said before filling her mouth with another bite of her mother's delicious pancakes.

Her mother's eyes narrowed slightly. "How did your visit to Wyndemere Academy go? I know you were worried about your event in the Youngling Games."

Fiona put down her fork. "You know that sports aren't really my thing, but I loved the library, and the class I took was really interesting. I met a lot of other Changers, too. Even a mermaid."

Mom looked concerned. "When the others found out you were a *selkie*, did they give you any trouble?"

"I didn't tell anyone I was a *selkie* princess, even though I'd like to tell the whole world that you're my mother," Fiona admitted. "The First Four said it was best to keep that secret, and after being at Wyndemere I can sort of see why."

"What happened?"

"The first two girls who learned I was a *selkie*—both waterborne Changers—didn't exactly make me feel welcome there. They thought I was a spy or something. Isn't that crazy?"

Mom sighed. "There's a lot of suspicion and distrust

between the *selkies* and the Changer nation at the moment. Old rumors have gotten blown way out of proportion, and what's going on between the finfolk and *selkies* in the Sea of Japan isn't helping matters. The other waterborne Changers have been keeping their distance from us, which is both a good thing and a bad thing. Good because it means less fighting. Bad because it means more suspicion. But you and I are going to change all of that soon." Mom squeezed her hand from across the table.

"Maybe I already started," Fiona said. "When they learned I was the *selkie* from Willow Cove, everything changed. I guess the four of us are pretty famous for defeating Auden Ironbound. And they knew that it was a *selkie* who destroyed his Horn of Power. All of a sudden they wanted to be friends, so that was kind of cool."

"It seems you've learned that actions really do speak louder than words," Mom said as she reached for another heap of pancakes. "Now tell me about the competition."

Fiona didn't want to worry her mother, but she couldn't avoid telling her about Sakura. "The competition never happened. The Shadow Fox put an end to that."

Mom didn't look quite as surprised as Fiona thought she would, but she urged her daughter to recount the full story about Mack's decision to confront Sakura, and Fiona's attempt to save him.

"She disappeared when I sang the Queen's Song, but not before she attacked Mack. And we're not sure exactly what she did to him. Mack can't remember, of course. We only know that she's trying to start a war."

Mom seemed to weigh her words carefully before she spoke. "You were very brave to go after your friend the way you did, but I want you to be more careful in the future. Sakura has powers that may be stronger than the Queen's Song."

Fiona's forehead wrinkled with confusion. "I thought the Queen's Song was the most powerful magic there is?"

"It's a powerful piece of *good* magic," her mother answered. "But there are things about dark magic that we'll likely never know—not without delving into dark magic ourselves. And that isn't safe. It was dark magic that turned Sakura into the Shadow Fox."

Fiona suspected there was something her mother

wasn't telling her. "Have you ever had any trouble with Sakura? Have the *selkies*?"

Mom turned and looked out the window, back toward her home on the Isles of Saorsie. "Sakura tried to force us into forming an alliance with her. She's amassing an army to fight the First Four and overthrow the Changer nation. She asked for our help. When we refused, she tried to use dark magic against us."

"What happened?" Fiona asked.

Mom shook her head. "We kept her at bay. She should know that *selkie* lands are protected against non-*selkies*. But there's concern that she's trying to find a way past our protections.

"I was afraid she might come after you and your friends. The council was against me using *selkie* magic in Changer-controlled areas, but I protected a few more places against non-*selkie* magical beings—this house and the stretch of beach below. Other than *selkies*, whom we know we can trust, no other magical beings will be able to enter this area."

For a moment Fiona felt safe and protected by her mother. Then she realized what those words really meant. "But, Mom!" she cried. "My friends, my teacher—They won't be able to come over!"

Having friends was a new experience for Fiona. The other kids at school were always nice, and she hadn't been bullied or anything like that, but she'd never had a best friend, either. When she learned she was a *selkie*, she, Mack, Darren, and Gabriella had become fast friends. She hated to think that now there was going to be a barrier between them.

"I'm sorry, Fiona, but this is for the best. And it's temporary. As soon as Sakura is contained, I'll lift the protections."

"I could have asked the First Four to work protection magic on the house. That way my friends could still come over," Fiona said.

But Mom wouldn't hear it. "*Selkie* magic is stronger than other forms of Changer magic. Nothing can harm you while you're here. And now that we know Sakura is after your friend, I know I was right to be worried about you."

Fiona was about to ask her mother to reconsider when she heard the rumble of the school bus. "I have to go," she said, grabbing her backpack. "I'll see you on Saturday."

Mom drew her into a hug. "Be safe, my girl."

Fiona caught a few glimpses of Mack in between classes. He still looked tired, but more like himself. By the time Fiona made it to the afternoon Changers class, she was happy to see that Mack was having fun racing Gabriella around the track for warm-ups. The two of them skidded to a stop a few feet ahead of Fiona and Changed back to their human forms.

"How are you suddenly so fast?" Gabriella asked, sounding almost winded.

"Practice makes perfect?" Mack responded with a smile. "Hey, Darren! Since I've tired out Gabriella, want to go another round at elemental archery? I never did get to crush you in the Youngling Games."

"Oh, you're so on," Darren retorted.

While Darren ran to set up the targets, Mack turned to Fiona and got serious for a moment. "By the way, Fiona, thanks for what you said yesterday. . . . I feel better knowing that maybe I did do something brave, and that's where my mystery tail came from. I was feeling kind of hopeless, and now I don't feel so bad anymore."

"I'm glad," Fiona said. "And I meant it."

Ms. Therian clapped her hands to get their attention. "Gather 'round! I want to introduce a new exercise we're going to try today."

There was an audible groan from Darren, upset that his chance to show Mack up at elemental archery was cut short once again.

Ms. Therian ignored him and pressed on. "As I think you all know by now, teamwork is a vital part of any mission. Successful training isn't just about honing your skills; it's also about finding ways to combine those skills with that of your teammates'." She turned toward the gym's double doors. "Please come in, Akira," she said.

Mack's grandfather entered the room, followed by a tall man who seemed to be made entirely out of shadow. The image startled Fiona for a moment, bringing her back to the Shadow Fox and the tower at Wyndemere.

"Don't be alarmed," Mr. Kimura said, sensing their unease. "This is just an illusion. I've conjured it for the purpose of this exercise. The instant one of you touches it"—Mr. Kimura waved a hand through the image—"it will disappear." The shadow dissolved.

"Your goal will be to use your powers and those of your teammates to catch the illusion. I'll be timing you. We'll run a few of these drills today, and maybe up the ante in a few days once you have the gist of it."

The four young Changers lined up along the indoor track, cracking knuckles and stretching muscles. Then with a flash, all had transformed except Fiona, who was humming an otherworldly tune. Ms. Therian blew her whistle, and they were off.

Gabriella broke ahead of the pack quickly, nearly catching the illusion within the first ten seconds. Darren tossed a few bolts haphazardly, trying to slow it down. Meanwhile, Fiona stayed behind, not even trying to catch up. Her humming turned into the tide song, and she made the hand motions her mother had taught her as she turned her attention to the saltwater pool. Summoning a wave from the ocean was easy. *Building* a wave in the pool required concentration and time.

But something strange was nagging at Fiona's concentration—it sounded like a snarl echoing from across the room, followed by a deep-throated growl. Who was doing that? Fiona opened her eyes for a moment and saw Mack. Something was off about his face—he looked fearful—like he was ready to attack, but that couldn't be right. They were just running a drill; no one was in any real danger.

Fiona got to the final crescendo of the tide song, and the wave symbol appeared on her palm. Pushing her hand forward on the last note, just like her mother had taught her, she watched as the wave burst out of the water, like a four-story wall, and crash down in the illusion's direction. The shadow man leaped out of the way, clearing the water with a superhuman jump. Before Fiona even had time to blink, Gabriella had used the distraction to close the distance between herself and the target.

Fiona watched Gabriella turn and prepare to pounce, but just at that moment, Mack jumped in front of Gabriella with a snarl.

Fiona gasped. *He's not snarling at the shadow; he's snarling at Gabriella!*

And then he lunged at her.

Chapter 4
The First Lesson

Instinctively, Gabriella dodged Mack's attack. She heard Fiona's startled scream behind her and then circled and stood her ground. She kept her eyes locked on Mack's, her weight on her front paws, ready to fight if she had to.

In her *nahual* form, Gabriella was hyperaware of everything around her. She realized that it wasn't her friend Mack she was squaring off against. She could hear his heart hammering in his chest, his eyes angry, his jaw clenched. Then he opened his *kitsune* mouth to show her his sharp teeth.

What is going on? Gabriella thought. *He's looking at me the same way he looks at our enemies.*

In a flash, the shadow illusion disappeared. Mr. Kimura transformed and jumped between Gabriella and his grandson. He growled at the younger *kitsune*, and Mack seemed to snap out of it. Looking from Gabriella to his grandfather in confusion, he pinned his ears back and sat down on the gym floor.

Darren transformed back into human form and cautiously approached the group. "What was that?"

"Are you all right?" Fiona asked Gabriella.

Gabriella only nodded, still in her *nahual* form. She didn't dare take her eyes off Mack. She was waiting for him to Change back, ready to protect Fiona and herself if she needed to.

When Mack Changed, the confusion in his eyes turned to fear. "I—I don't know what came over me," Mack stammered. "I felt this surge of adrenaline, and I'm not really sure what happened next. I felt like I was in danger, and the next thing I knew I was in attack mode. I couldn't control it. Gabriella, you have to understand—"

Mack tried to move toward her, but Mr. Kimura blocked his way. Then Mack noticed his friends' frightened faces. "I would never have . . . ," he whispered.

In a flash, Gabriella Changed back to her human form. "It's all right," she told him, relaxing a bit. "I know you wouldn't have bitten me. It just caught me off guard."

Mack's eyes filled with tears. Then he hung his head, shame replacing fear.

Mr. Kimura transformed and put a hand on Mack's shoulder. "Come, Makoto," he said. "Let us talk."

Gabriella watched the two of them walk to the other side of the gym and begin a quiet conversation in Japanese. She could tell even from across the room that Mack was trying very hard not to cry, and suddenly, Gabriella was swallowing tears of her own.

That wasn't him! she thought desperately. She knew deep down that only really powerful dark magic could cause Mack to turn on one of his friends. *He would never have done anything like that before Sakura bit him. What did she do to him?*

"I think we'll cut practice short today," Ms. Therian said. "We all need a break. We'll continue training for your mission tomorrow—be sure to bring your questions about the mission brief." She sent Gabriella, Fiona, and Darren to the locker rooms to clean up.

While Fiona showered off the salt water from the pool, Gabriella splashed cold water on her face at the sink. She was still shaken about what had happened, replaying the incident over and over in her head.

Would Mack really have attacked me? What if his grandfather hadn't come between us and gotten him to back down?

"Do you think Sakura could be controlling Mack?" she asked Fiona suddenly.

Fiona grabbed a towel and started to dry off. "I don't know," she said. "At Wyndemere, those high school kids told us that Sakura could use memory eating to turn friends on one another. I thought our bond was too strong for that, but . . ." Her voice trailed off.

"It is," Gabriella said fiercely. She needed to believe in that connection more than anyone if she was to have a chance at saving Mack.

Fiona nodded. "Sorry—you're right. And for the record, I don't believe Mack would have really attacked you in the end. The real Mack would have stepped in and stopped himself before things got too bad. The good in him is stronger than whatever Sakura left behind. . . .

"But it was really scary," Fiona went on. "Anyway, I'm sure the First Four will find a solution or a cure for whatever's going on with Mack soon. With all the magic in the world, there has to be a way."

Gabriella didn't tell Fiona that her spirit-walking ability was *supposed* to be the cure. Mack's grandfather had asked her to keep it a secret. But Gabriella felt more and more like maybe keeping Darren and Fiona out of the loop was a mistake. If the four friends really did share a bond, didn't secrets like this just weaken it?

After track practice, Gabriella headed home for her first lesson in spirit-walking. Her mother would be at work until later, and Maritza had gone to a friend's house after school. Tía Rosa had returned to New Brighton for the day, but promised she'd be back soon. Gabriella and her grandmother had the house to themselves.

Gabriella quickly filled Abuelita in on her frightening experience in the gym. "It's more important than ever that I learn how to do this," she said.

Abuelita gave her a hug. "But it can't be rushed, *mija*.

There are things you need to learn before you even attempt to spirit-walk again. You'll be at risk of losing yourself if you don't."

"Losing myself?" Gabriella shivered at the thought. *What does that mean, really? What would be left of me if my spirit got lost in the dreamworld—or in Mack's brain? Just a shell?*

Afraid to hear the full answer, she only asked, "Where do we start?"

"The first thing you have to master is meditation," Abuelita said gently. "That's easier said than done, but I know you can do it." She led Gabriella to a cushion she had set up in Gabriella's bedroom.

"Sit quietly and focus on your breathing," she explained. "You want to free your mind of thoughts until it's just you and the breathing."

Gabriella tried and failed, and tried and failed, again and again. "I keep thinking thoughts," she said, growing frustrated. "Why was this so easy the first time, when I spirit-walked in Darren's dreams? I didn't have to meditate."

"It's possible that Yara put your mind in the right

place first," Abuelita explained. "That was an emergency situation, but you'll be stronger and more protected if you can learn to do it yourself."

But after another few minutes of failed attempts, Gabriella threw her hands in the air. "I don't think I'm getting it," she said in exasperation. "Thoughts keep bouncing around in my head. I keep picturing Mack lunging for me and hearing Fiona scream."

"Patience. Meditation is all about having a relaxed mind. At your age that's hard to accomplish, especially with everything that's been going on. But I know you'll get there."

Gabriella nodded. "I'll try, but I'm not so sure."

"When thoughts come in, I want you to imagine yourself breathing them out with your exhale. Then come back to focusing on the breath when you inhale," Abuelita said. "Soon, your thoughts will quiet, and you'll be able to focus solely on your meditation.

"Think about your transformation, about how it is as effortless as breathing, how you become aware of every part of your *nahual* body," she continued. "Use that same awareness to maintain focus."

Gabriella nodded again and tried to do what her grandmother suggested.

"Good," Abuelita said in a soothing tone. "Now breathe in and out. In and out." She breathed along with Gabriella for a moment. "Feel your muscles relax, but keep your mind open to the energy that flows through all living things."

Gabriella started to feel it, as if she was letting go of everything except the energy of the world. She felt embraced by it, like the energy was becoming a part of her, and she a part of it. It was so peaceful! If she wanted to, Gabriella felt like she could give up control and let the energy pick her up and carry her off. She was about to see what that would be like when a hand on her shoulder jolted her out of the meditation.

Gabriella blinked, coming back into the room, feeling the pillow and the floor beneath her and Abuelita's hand on her shoulder. She still felt deeply at peace and wanted to reenter the meditation. It was so calm and relaxing after what had happened at school earlier.

"Be careful, *mija*. It's important that you hold on to your sense of self," her grandmother warned. "There's a fine line between being fully relaxed in meditation and losing your tether to this world. It's a skill you must master. If you let go completely, your spirit could become lost."

Gabriella's peace was shattered by a jolt of adrenaline. "Wait—it could happen like that? Without me even realizing it?"

Abuelita nodded gravely. "Why did you think this training usually takes years to master? But don't worry; knowing that feeling—the feeling of letting go—is half the battle. Now you'll know to pull back when you reach that point."

Gabriella shook her head. "I thought I was finally getting it."

"You were," Abuelita reassured her. "I want you to remember what that deep meditation felt like. That's the state you need to be in before you spirit-walk. But if you ever feel like you're drifting off, you need to have the strength to pull back. That takes practice."

"Okay, let's try it again," Gabriella said with a shaky sigh.

"I think we've done enough for today," Abuelita answered. "You need a break, and I promised your mother I'd make my famous huevos rancheros for breakfast tomorrow, so I need to go grab some things from the store."

Grocery shopping at a time like this? Gabriella thought.

"But I really want to keep going," Gabriella blurted out.

"I'm sorry, *mija*, but you need to rest. I know you're in a hurry, but rushing this part of the training is dangerous. Once you have this down we'll speed things up, I promise."

"But how can I think about normal things like shopping and breakfast when everyone's counting on me?"

Abuelita smiled and stood, ruffling Gabriella's hair. "Breakfast in this house is *never* normal, magic or no magic. And someday you will learn that if you only focus on saving the world, you'll forget just what it is you're saving. Spending time with your family—even if it's just for a *normal* breakfast—is important for both yourself and your training. It strengthens your tether to this world."

Abuelita turned to go, but stopped in the doorway. "You know, I very much enjoy spending this special time with you. You're a lot less whiny than your aunt was at your age."

Gabriella laughed. "Do you need any help tonight?"

"Not with the shopping, but you can chop the onions in the morning," she said. Then she left Gabriella alone.

Gabriella let out a huge breath that she hadn't realized she'd been holding in. It would be dinnertime soon, and then bed, and then another day, another Changers class in which she had to face Mack.

I get what Abuelita is saying, but I still feel like I should be doing more—training harder, Gabriella thought. *Whatever's going on with Mack is getting worse, and I'm just sitting here, no closer to spirit-walking than I was before. What if they need me to spirit-walk tomorrow? There's no way I'd be ready.*

As if on cue, her cell phone chimed with an incoming text from Mack.

Sorry about today. Dont know what came over me.

Gabriella texted back:

Im fine. You ok?

freaked out before but better now . . . sometimes my thoughts are sort of out of my control. I dont know what to do.

what do you mean?

it's like I feel scrambled and then something inside me takes over. Something mean. Like Im on autopilot and barely remember what I did or said after. Im scared I could hurt you guys.

Gabriella felt that pang of guilt hit her again, full force. Here was Mack, her friend who so deeply believed in her and her abilities from the start and who now so desperately needed her.

What could she possibly say to reassure him, when she herself was worried out of her mind?

It's gonna be ok. The first four will figure out what's going on, and my spirit-walking lessons are going great. I learned how to meditate on my own tonight, and I've got another lesson tomorrow. You and me, we're going to beat Sakura.

Gabriella watched her screen flicker a few times, as though Mack was typing a response and then erasing it, typing and erasing. Finally, a text came through.

Yeah. Thanks for understanding. Night

Gabriella wasn't convinced by Mack's response. She wasn't even convinced by her own words that the lessons were "going great." She put her arms behind her head and tried to focus on her breathing, so she could push away how anxious and unsettled she was.

Chapter 5
A Normal Afternoon

Darren left school after Changers class on Friday relieved that Mack hadn't had another episode like he'd had earlier in the week. Mack didn't seem *exactly* like himself—he was more than a little guarded—but he had performed well in all the training exercises Ms. Therian had thrown at them. Everyone, especially Mack, was relieved that there wasn't a repeat of Tuesday's events.

Now Darren was looking forward to a normal Saturday afternoon like any other twelve-year-old. Pizza, video games, maybe a movie.

Darren had been one of the most popular kids at Willow Cove Middle School for as long as he could remember, but he could never really figure out why. He'd always tried to do what his big brother, Ray, had done in school—be nice, no matter what anyone else said or did or thought. Darren was sure he'd never admit it to Ray, but he looked up to him a lot.

Darren longed to tell Ray about his life as a Changer, but he wasn't sure his big brother would understand. Ray had helped Darren through so much, especially since their parents decided to get a divorce, but finding out that his little bro could transform into a giant bird and shoot lightning from his talons?

That would probably be a lot to take in, Darren thought. *Even for the most supportive big brother in the world.*

Darren may have wished he could share his Changer secret with his brother, but he was still pretty sure he never wanted his friends at school to know. He'd been best friends with Ethan Renner and Kyle Rodriguez since they were all in preschool, and he knew the two of them better than anyone. He could just imagine how telling them would go over. . . .

Could you give us a lift to school? Get it? A lift. 'Cause you're a bird!

Maybe you could zap the school's power out so we don't have to go to math class today. They unlocked the expansion pack for Space Alien Hunters 4 last night, so I didn't have time to study for that math quiz.

Nah. Darren would definitely prefer to keep his secret powers under wraps when it came to his friends. But that was fine; Darren had Mack, Fiona, and Gabriella to talk to about Changer stuff.

Darren decided to sleep in Saturday morning and woke up to a string of text messages from Ethan and Kyle. They were headed to the movies that afternoon and wanted Darren to join them.

It had been way too long since Darren had hung out with them outside of track practice. Actually, it had been way too long since he'd hung out with anyone his own age that wasn't talking about shadow foxes and ancient curses and the "coming war."

Darren didn't have to meet the Changers for their mission in Japan until after dinner that night. There was definitely time to go to the movies and get to the school before then. Luckily, Darren had already cleared the Japan operation with his mom. . . . Or rather, Mr.

Kimura had told Darren's mom that Darren would be at Mack's house for a game night and wouldn't be home until later.

Darren clumped down the stairs and found his mother in the kitchen. "Can I go to the movies with Ethan and Kyle this afternoon?" he asked. "Kyle's dad is going to drop us off and pick us up."

"I don't see why not," she said. "Text me Kyle's dad's number?"

"Definitely," Darren said, rattling off the number in a text to his mom. Then he sent a new message to Kyle and Ethan to tell them he was up for going to the movies and ran upstairs to get ready. It wasn't long before he heard a car horn beeping from the street below his bedroom window.

"Darren?" Kyle said in an faux old man voice when he hopped into the car. "Could that really be you? How long has it been? Three, four hundred years?"

"Ha-ha," Darren retorted, punching his friend in the arm. "I ate lunch with you yesterday, turd."

"Yeah, but outside of school and track, you've been MIA, dude," Ethan added. "Which reminds me, did you talk to Gabriella about ice cream with Trisha and Reese after the track meet next Saturday?"

"She never texted me back, but I'm sure it's okay."

"And I'm sure it will be *twooo wuv* between you and Reese," Kyle added in baby talk.

Ethan elbowed him in the ribs as the car pulled up to the movie theater. The friends hopped out of the car, thanked Kyle's dad, and headed inside.

"Remember that karate class we all took when we were five?" Darren asked, pointing to a movie poster for an upcoming martial arts film beside the ticket booth.

"The best thing about it," Ethan said, "was being able to take our shoes off and stick our feet in other people's faces."

Darren cracked up. "Dude, every time you took your shoes off, a green haze settled over the room."

"Be careful, or I'll take my shoes off now," Ethan joked.

"Don't make us faint before the movie!" Kyle cried.

Soon, they had moved on to talking about the "movies" they had made in third grade. Kyle had gotten a small video camera for Christmas, and the three of them had taken roles as superheroes battling evil villains, cavemen running from dinosaurs, and aliens determined to invade Willow Cove in a whole series of films they thought were great at the time.

What would they think about me battling real villains? Darren wondered.

He watched his friends demonstrate a human versus dinosaur fight they had thought was Academy Award–worthy when they were seven. Laughing along with Kyle and Ethan made Darren realize how much he missed hanging out with his old friends.

I *miss the days when my biggest worries had to do with surprise pop quizzes, rain on my* Little League *games, and whether or not* Becky Jenkins *was going to check yes or no on my note asking whether she liked me.* Now *I'm worried about evil shape-shifters and a magical war.*

But even with all the Changers stuff going on, Darren saw the importance in hanging out with his friends: It reminded him that there were people in this world that Darren was fighting to protect. Goofy memories and silly jokes and "wasting time" messing around with friends . . . These were the reasons why the world was worth saving in the first place. Why Sakura, with her twisted view of the world, could never win. And even if it was only for the length of the movie, Darren was determined to savor every minute of being a thoroughly normal seventh-grader with his extraordinarily average friends.

By the middle of the film, a dumb but hilarious spy comedy, their popcorn bucket was empty and Darren decided to head out for a refill. He was waiting for the clerk at the counter when a woman came toward him, walking fast. Before Darren knew what was happening, she was throwing firebolts his way.

Darren raised his hands and fell back, concentrating on letting sparks form at his fingertips. Those sparks joined together, creating a glowing web of electricity. Then he waved his arms to form a circle that included himself and the clerk behind the concession counter.

The force field repelled the flames, but the woman kept coming. Her firebolts hit his force field and recoiled, shooting right back at her, but it was as though she was immune to the flames.

She smiled at Darren. "You'll tire soon," she said. "I can wait."

Darren concentrated on holding his electric bubble in place, but she was right. He was already feeling exhausted. Holding a force field took a tremendous amount of energy, but he didn't know if he had the skills to fight her, either.

He tried to keep his focus on her and not on the movie theater employee who was totally freaked out. At least the guy was frozen with fear and too scared to scream. The last thing Darren needed was a distraction.

Suddenly, two men burst out of the theater and got in between Darren and the woman. Darren realized he had seen them on the street earlier that day, but thought nothing of it. Now he prepared for the worst, but instead of attacking *him*, the men went after his attacker.

The fight was so fast, Darren's head spun. The enemy was clearly losing when she transformed into a *phoenix*, a firebird, and crashed through the theater's front window to get away.

Darren let go of his force field and collapsed, feeling like he had just been kicked in the stomach. The first man helped Darren to his feet while the other snapped his fingers. The passersby on the street who had been gawking at the window and the bird a moment before turned their heads and kept on walking like nothing had happened. Another second after that, Darren watched as the pieces of glass started to float together. Soon, the window was fixed. There was no evidence that it had ever been smashed.

In the meantime, the man who had helped Darren get to his feet was standing in front of the concession stand and singing an eerie song to the guy behind the counter. It sounded a lot like a song Yara had once sung when she and Fiona were talking about the differences between *encantados* and *selkies*. The guy behind the counter went from looking scared out of his mind to happy and oblivious. The *encantado* had wiped the guy's memories of the whole terrifying event.

Then the *encantado* drew Darren away from the refreshment counter so they could talk without being overheard. The clerk hummed as he restocked candy.

"Are you all right?" the *encantado* asked Darren.

Darren nodded. "Thanks to you two. Who are you?"

"We're part of your protection detail."

"My protection what?" Darren asked blankly.

"The First Four didn't— Surely you must've assumed?" the *encantado* asked.

Darren shook his head.

"Until Sakura is eliminated as a threat, the First Four want to make sure that you and your friends stay safe," he explained. "We weren't supposed to make ourselves known unless there was a definite threat."

"I guess that was a definite threat," Darren said, taking a deep, shaky breath.

The other man had gone outside and was looking up and down the street. Satisfied that there was no one else about to attack, he joined them. "We're clear," he said.

"I thought I saw you both on my way into the movie theater. Are you following me everywhere?" Darren asked.

"You're protected by Changer magic at home and at school. We follow you when you leave those safe areas," the second man said. "When you're out in the world, we'll be shadowing you—from a distance, of course."

"So that was—"

"One of Sakura's," the man cut in. "Try not to think about it too much. You're perfectly safe."

Darren had a lot more questions, but his protectors brought an end to the conversation.

"You should rejoin your friends before they come looking for you and start asking questions," the *encantado* said.

Darren nodded, still a little dazed—both by the attack and the fact he now had this Changer version of the Secret Service following him around. It made everything seem much more dangerous than it had just that morning.

After a very awkward thank-you, he headed back into the theater.

"What did I miss?" he whispered.

"The funny spy is now the mean spy, and vice versa," Kyle whispered back. "And they're both too dumb to figure out that the bad guy is right in front of them."

"Hey, dude, where's the popcorn?" Ethan asked.

Darren shrugged. "There was no one at the concession stand. I waited for a while, and then I gave up. Sorry."

"You're the worst," Kyle said sarcastically, receiving an instant punch in the arm from Darren.

Darren settled back into his seat, but he couldn't

concentrate on the movie anymore. He pretended to laugh along with his friends, but he couldn't pretend to himself that everything was back to normal, that he was back to normal, even for an afternoon.

I'm part of the next generation of the First Four, he thought. *My life will never be normal again.*

Chapter 6
The Labyrinth

That night, Fiona waited for Mr. Kimura and the others to pick her up and take her to the gym. They wouldn't be able to enter the driveway because of her mother's protections, so she stood at the end of the front walkway to avoid having any awkward conversations.

Fiona took a deep breath and thought about what she had read in their mission folder. There weren't a lot of details about what they hoped to find or exactly where they were going. Fiona knew only that they were on the lookout for magical objects, talismans that would protect them from the Shadow Fox's attempts at mind control, and that this one was somewhere in Japan.

I suppose it makes sense that the First Four would be sparse on the details, she thought. *If the mission brief fell into the wrong hands, we could be intercepted by Sakura's forces.* Though Fiona had a sneaking suspicion that Sakura's forces would find a way to intercept them no matter what.

Fiona was glad that Gabriella now carried the Ring of Tezcatlipoca with her all the time. And of course Fiona had her Queen's Song for protection. The sooner they found talismans to keep Mack and Darren safe, the better.

Mr. Kimura's car pulled up. Fiona expected to see Mack in the front seat as usual, but instead, Gabriella sat up front with Mr. Kimura. Darren waved from the back. *Maybe Mack's already at the school,* she thought.

Fiona hopped into the backseat beside Darren. She was about to ask where Mack was when Gabriella turned to her.

"Can you believe they attacked Darren in broad daylight like that?!"

Fiona was confused. "Wait—who attacked?"

"You didn't get my message?" Darren asked.

Fiona shook her head. "My phone died. I just turned it back on a few minutes ago." With that, Fiona whipped out her phone, only to discover a thread of unread messages from Darren and Gabriella. Mack was on the text too, but he hadn't said anything either.

"Sakura sent a *phoenix* after me," he said. "But it turned out all right . . . thanks to the First Four's protection squad. I'm not sure I could have held that Changer off on my own."

"Protection squad?" Fiona asked.

Darren filled her in on his unexpected rescue.

"So then . . . do we all have Changers following us?" Fiona asked.

Mr. Kimura nodded. "All four of you have guards whenever you're in an unsecured area. Ms. Therian and I made sure that your homes have been enchanted with protective magic. Except Fiona's—the *selkies* took care of that before we got there."

Fiona looked sheepishly out the window.

"And, of course, the school is safe for you. But whenever you leave one of those areas and aren't with a member of the First Four, you'll have guards. They'll stay at a distance. You may not even see them, but you can trust that they're there, ready to step in if needed. Darren discovered that today."

He parked in front of the entrance to the middle school's ancillary gym, and they went inside. Once again, Fiona noticed Mack's absence, but just as she tried to ask Mr. Kimura about Mack for a second time, two old friends joined them.

Miles Campagna, the *aatxe*, or magical bull, who had helped them locate Circe's Compass for their battle with Auden Ironbound's forces, greeted them with a smile. Fiona was happy to see him again.

The other familiar face was that of Margaery Haruyama, a *tengu* Changer who could control the wind. The *tengu* had the power to transport them anywhere in the world in the blink of an eye. She had transported Fiona and her friends to Wyndemere Academy for the Youngling Games, and Fiona hoped she would be joining them on this trip as well. She was happy to see that her hunch was right.

After they exchanged greetings, Mr. Kimura asked them to sit for a debriefing.

"We didn't want to include too many details in your mission folders in case they fell into the wrong hands, but now I can tell you that our mission is to recover a very special *magatama* talisman," he said. "*Magatama* were meant to bring good fortune to their wearers and to ward off evil."

He conjured a picture of the *magatama* for them to see. It was a comma-shaped pendant that was looped by a piece of string and made of curved stone that appeared to be a dark jade.

"It's beautiful," Fiona said.

"Beautiful and precious. This talisman can be used to protect Makoto from Sakura's memory eating if we can retrieve it," Mr. Kimura said. "This mission could be very dangerous. I have no doubt that Sakura's forces also know of the *magatama*'s existence and what it can do to protect Makoto. They'll be searching for it too. And they'll want to keep us from it."

"Do you think they know where it is?" Gabriella asked.

"*We're* not even positive where it is," Mr. Kimura answered. "We recently came across some new information that indicates the necklace is hidden on a northern Japanese island called Hokkaido," Mr. Kimura answered. "That's where we'll search tonight, or shall I say this morning— With the time difference it's currently eight a.m. in Hokkaido. Are there any questions before we begin?"

Where's Mack? Fiona thought. She could tell by the way they eyed each other that Gabriella and Darren had the same question, but none of them wanted to be the one to ask. Mr. Kimura was already torn up about what Sakura had done to his grandson. *Asking will only make him feel worse,* Fiona realized.

But Mr. Kimura had the wisdom to know what they were thinking. "Makoto will not be joining us tonight," he said. "I thought it was best for him to remain under magical protection until he has the talisman."

Then he turned to the *tengu*. "If you would, Margaery," he said with a nod. "It's time."

The group stood in a circle with Margaery at the center and rested their palms on her shoulders.

I wonder if going all the way to Japan will take two blinks— Before Fiona even completed the thought, the group was on its way.

There was a whoosh, and for a moment, Fiona felt like she was nestled inside the calm heart of the wind. For two or three dizzying seconds the world flew by, and then they landed gently in what appeared to be a forest. It was damp, the trees were dense, and the air was sharp and cold with the spicy smell of pine. Fiona pictured the world map that hung on the wall in her advanced geography class and remembered that Japan stretched as far north as Russia. *No wonder it's colder here than in Willow Cove*, she thought.

Mr. Kimura walked ahead and cleared a path for them. He was followed by Darren, Gabriella, and Miles. Fiona and Margaery took up the rear. The sun was up, but it filtered weakly through the dense pines. The group traveled quietly, so as not to attract any unwanted attention.

"How are there still enchanted objects like this *magatama* talisman just laying around where Sakura and her followers might be able to find them?" Fiona whispered to Margaery. "I mean, if Changers have been looking for magical relics for years, shouldn't they all have been found by now?"

"The world is a big place," Margaery answered. "During the Time of the Dark, many Changers hid their most prized possessions, especially the magical ones. They used cloaking spells to try to keep them out of the hands of humans and warlocks."

The Time of the Dark. It wasn't just the cold that made Fiona shiver. She had first heard about the Time of the Dark from the Changers' magical book, *The Compendium*, and she'd pieced together the rest from the First Four and her visits to the library at Wyndemere. Changer- and magic-kind hadn't always led secret lives. They used to live openly in partnership with normal humans. But a thousand years ago, a dangerous warlock used the Horn of Power—the same Horn of Power that Fiona herself had destroyed—to turn the Changers against nonmagical people. Even after the First Four defeated the warlock and locked away the horn, the damage had been done. Nonmagical beings banished the Changers from their villages, or worse, hunted them down.

That was the beginning of the Time of the Dark, when the Changers had been forced to create a hidden world. For hundreds of years Changers lived apart from humans in hidden Changer bases. But gradually, they moved back into the wider world, living side by side with non-Changers once again. They continued to do what they could to protect mankind. Even so, they had no choice but to do it in secret.

"But it's been centuries since the Time of the Dark," Fiona said. "Why haven't the magical talismans been found before now?"

"As Changers disappeared or died, their secrets went with them," Margaery answered. "Finding and reclaiming these objects has been a priority for the current First Four for hundreds of years. But most relics are deeply hidden and protected by magic. We many never find everything the ancients left behind."

Fiona was fascinated by the idea of powerful talismans hidden all over the world. She was about to ask Margaery if she knew anything about *selkie* relics when Mr. Kimura announced that they had arrived at their destination.

He stepped into a clearing in the forest and waved his hand over the ground. As he did so, a hidden stone pathway appeared. The stones led to what appeared to be a dark, mossy circle. As Fiona neared, she saw that it was a hole.

We're headed underground, down into the earth.

The team wound their way through a series of underground tunnels. Both Mr. Kimura and Margaery cast spells to light their way. Chambers off the sides of the tunnels revealed silver coins, shiny lacquered boxes inlaid with mother of pearl, and ancient samurai armor.

Fiona would have loved to explore it all, but Mr. Kimura kept up a steady pace.

With Sakura's forces looking for us, there's no time to lose, but I want to come back and explore here one day . . . , she thought. *Someone needs to put together a complete history of Changers and to map the lost places like this. Maybe I can be the one to do that.*

Fiona was beginning to feel comfortable with the dark and eerie quiet of the underground world, when Mr. Kimura communicated to them telepathically. *Don't touch anything; these objects are enchanted against intruders—there's no telling what could happen. And be as quiet as you can. I don't believe we're alone here.*

The group continued through the maze of tunnels as

quietly as possible. Fiona was even afraid to breathe too deeply for fear of attracting the notice of one of Sakura's followers.

They had all just stepped into one corridor when a hairy creature burst out of it with an eerie screech. Fiona nearly screamed, but Mr. Kimura simply waved his hand and muttered under his breath. The creature disappeared.

It was an illusion to keep us away, Fiona realized.

One corridor that looked promising led them to a steep rock wall, blocking them from going farther. They turned back to the main tunnel, which led them to another corridor and a deep pool.

This is probably another dead end, Mr. Kimura thought to them. *Fiona, can you explore the pool?*

Fiona drew her *selkie* cloak around her and dove into the water. It was blacker than any water she had ever seen, even deep in the ocean. She waited a moment for her eyes to adjust, but it was still too dark. She surfaced.

Can you conjure some kind of light? I think the water is enchanted to keep me from seeing anything.

Mr. Kimura nodded and whispered a few words in Japanese.

Fiona dove under again, and this time there was a faint glow in the water, allowing her to see. And that's when she saw them—sharks swimming all around her. They were coming toward her with their mouths open wide. Fiona nearly jumped out of the water when she realized something.

There's no way this many sharks could live in such a small pool. This is another illusion!

Steeling her courage, she forced herself to let them swim right for her. The lead shark opened its mouth wide, as if to bite her, but she felt nothing. She would have laughed if she wasn't afraid of making a noise.

The sharks forgotten, she circled the pool. She swam as close as possible to the smooth rock wall, searching for an opening or a door of some kind. Finding nothing, she dove to the bottom and searched there, again finding nothing.

You were right, she communicated to Mr. Kimura as she hopped out of the water and removed her cloak. *A dead end.*

They made their way back to the main tunnel once again. After the next turn, their path took a steep downward pitch. The air was noticeably colder. *How far underground are we?* Fiona wondered. *How long will we be able to breathe this air?*

But the next thing she knew, they had stepped into a chamber. It was bigger than most of the others and held the group comfortably and with room to spare. There were shelves on the walls with ancient katana, a type of Japanese sword, and other objects. In the center of one wall was a *magatama* necklace—a real version of the one that Mr. Kimura had conjured for them earlier. He motioned for the group to form a semicircle behind him.

Fiona stood between Gabriella and Darren with Margaery and Miles at either end. They watched Mack's grandfather approach the talisman with cautious respect. He bowed with his hands clasped in front of him, whispering some sort of spell. The jade talisman glowed for a moment, and then Mr. Kimura performed another spell. He spoke so quietly that Fiona didn't hear the words, but she gasped when the necklace practically jumped off the wall and into his hands. He bowed three times and slipped the necklace into his pocket.

And now—just as silently—we must leave as quickly as we can, Mr. Kimura communicated.

The small group turned to leave.

But there, standing in the doorway, was another team of Changers.

Chapter 7
The Magatama

Darren recognized the *phoenix* who had attacked him at the movie theater. She was accompanied by three others. He remembered Mr. Kimura's words about the enchanted objects and cast a force field around the shelves and the magical items on the walls before Sakura's followers accidentally set off some ancient protective spell that would endanger them all.

Good thinking, Darren, Mr. Kimura thought to him.

Darren had a moment to feel proud before the room descended into chaos. Mr. Kimura answered the flamethrower's fiery arrows with flames his own. The hurricane-force wind Margaery created held the three other Changers at bay. They struggled against it, but it held them in the doorway. They couldn't get past it and into the chamber.

But then one of them did—a man transformed into a giant werewolf, let loose a powerful roar, and pushed his way through the wind. A *nykur*—a horse Changer—just behind him tried to break through on the werewolf's heels, but Margaery blew it backward again with her howling wind. It tumbled into a *naga*, a giant snake.

The werewolf headed straight for Gabriella.

Gabriella! Watch out! Darren communicated.

Gabriella had already transformed. Darren saw the Ring of Tezcatlipoca glittering on her front paw. Now she pounced on the werewolf, her sharp claws doing serious damage. Still, she was no match for the sheer size of the creature, and Miles rushed to her aid, his bull's head down, driving his horns into the creature and, together with Margaery's wind, pushing it back.

Darren struggled to keep his force field in place, but he could already feel himself weakening.

I *can't keep this up for much longer,* he thought to Mr. Kimura.

It's important that we don't set off the protection spells on the objects. Focus your power—we only need a few more minutes, Mr. Kimura answered.

Darren took a step back and reinforced the electric shield around the magical objects, but still his energy was waning. He cast his eyes around the room, searching for help.

Everyone was completely focused on battling Sakura's forces except for Fiona. *Why is she holding back?* he wondered.

Fiona! Darren communicated. I *need your help to keep them away from the objects—sing the Queen's Song.*

Darren knew that with the Queen's Song, Fiona could temporarily shut down the other Changers' magic, leaving them unable to fight. It would bring the battle to a close in seconds.

I *can't sing in such close quarters*, she answered.

Even though they were communicating telepathically, Darren could hear the frustration in her voice.

Everyone's too close together and moving too fast, she explained. I *can't focus on any one individual with the song.*

Sing to the whole room! Darren answered.

I *can't*, she said. *If* I *sing the Queen's Song in a room this small, it could knock you out too, or strip everyone of their magic. It's too dangerous.*

Darren was trying to think of another way for her to help them when he saw the *naga* break through Margaery's wind barrier. It reared up as if to bite Margaery.

Darren stepped in to fight by her side, and the force field broke. He felt it crackle before it disappeared in a shower of sparks. The *naga* whipped around in his direction and hit him right in the midsection with her thick snake's tail. Darren dropped to his knees, feeling as if the creature had sliced him in half.

Margaery jumped in front of him and took the monster on. But the *nykur* came to the *naga*'s aid. Mr. Kimura was busy with the *phoenix* while Gabriella and Miles battled the werewolf.

At the same time, with the collapse of the force field, the enchanted objects began to rocket around the room. They collided with people and with one another. One heavy sword fell from the ceiling to hit the werewolf on the head. The giant creature turned to swat the sword away, but the minute he touched it, he turned to stone. He was frozen, his paw still raised.

Back into the tunnel! Mr. Kimura told them. *I have the* magatama. *We must get away from the rest of the magical objects.*

He cast an illusion spell over each member of the Willow Cove team as they made their way back into the underground world's main tunnel.

The *phoenix* and the *naga* tried to follow, but Darren watched Margaery blow them deeper into the chamber. Then she cast a spell and ducked just in time before another sword dropped from the ceiling and knocked the flamethrower to the ground. She was unconscious.

Margaery joined the rest of them in the tunnel, and Mr. Kimura performed a spell to seal the chamber off. A solid stone rolled into place, blocking Sakura's forces from getting out.

"Should we run while we can? Before they figure out how to escape?" Darren asked out loud. "We've got the talisman."

Mr. Kimura shook his head. "We must capture them if we can," he answered. "But let's catch our breath and wait for the objects to settle down."

After a while, Gabriella, in her *nahual* form, put an

ear to the stone. *It's quiet in there now,* she said to the group.

Mr. Kimura and Margaery had a whispered conversation, and he asked the others to stand back. He opened the chamber while Margaery cast a spell.

Darren gasped when the stone slid away from the chamber's entrance. Enchanted objects still littered the floor, but they were beginning to reassemble and take their places on the shelves. He watched as a set of ancient katana righted themselves on the wall.

The werewolf was still frozen in stone, and the *phoenix* was still unconscious. He wondered why Mr. Kimura looked so concerned, but then Darren realized that the *naga* and the *nykur* had escaped.

Why would they leave their teammates behind? Darren wondered. *Were they afraid the curses would affect them, too, if they moved them?*

As if on cue, Margaery performed a spell on the two remaining members of Sakura's forces.

Darren almost laughed when he saw what it had done—the werewolf and the *phoenix* floated into the air as if they were completely weightless, and then

Margaery used a gentle wind to push them into the tunnel. The prisoners floated gently, bobbing up and down, as the entire group made their way out of the cave.

When they were back in the clearing in the forest, Mr. Kimura reenchanted the tomb. The dark hole seemed to fold in on itself. The entrance to the underground world was hidden and sealed off once again. Then the stone pathway beneath their feet disappeared.

"We must hurry home," Mr. Kimura said. "There may be more of Sakura's forces lurking nearby, and we don't know where the *nykur* and the *naga* are. They may have gone for reinforcements."

They each put a hand on Margaery—Mr. Kimura and Miles each holding on to a sleeve of one of Sakura's disabled and now weightless warriors—and in a blink, they were back inside Willow Cove Middle School's enchanted gym. Darren was exhausted but hopeful. They had the talisman. Finding it was the purpose of their mission. They had succeeded.

Soon, Mack will be free of Sakura's dark magic, he thought. *We'll be a solid team again.*

"Margaery and I will take these two to a holding

cell at the Harbor," Miles offered, taking hold of the Changer Mr. Kimura was holding. Both Changers still hovered over the ground. "They won't be giving us any more trouble. You can all call it a night."

"Thank you, Miles," Mr. Kimura said. "Thank you, Margaery. You have done good work tonight." Then he looked to the three seventh-graders. "You all have. Makoto and I are very grateful."

Mr. Kimura asked Darren, Fiona, and Gabriella if they would come back to the house with him. "I think you should be the ones to give Makoto the *magatama*. I know it will cheer him up to see you."

The small group arrived at the Kimura house to find Mack lying on the couch, watching a dumb comedy on television. Darren recognized the same actor he had seen on the movie theater screen earlier that day.

Mack clicked off the TV when they entered the room, but he didn't seem all that happy to see them. He wasn't even curious about what they had been doing.

He knew we were on the mission. Why isn't he asking us about it? Darren wondered.

"Excuse me, while I put the tea kettle on," Mr.

Kimura said. "I'll leave you with your friends, Makoto."

Mack dropped the remote control on the coffee table and sat up a little grudgingly.

"We missed you tonight," Fiona said, sitting next to him.

"The First Four didn't want me on the mission," he said with shrug. "They were worried about me after what happened in class during the training exercise the other day." He held Gabriella's eyes for a second and then looked away. "Like I might turn evil on all of you or something."

"That's ridiculous," Gabriella said. "You wouldn't have hurt us."

Mack shrugged again, but Darren could tell he wasn't as indifferent as he was pretending to be. He was hiding his hurt and his fear.

"They don't trust me anymore," Mack said, bitterness creeping into his voice. "They didn't want me there to help you. They didn't want me to visit my parents' birthplace.

"We didn't see anything of Japan—unless you count an underground cave—but the mission was a success," Darren said. "We brought you back something—a talisman that will protect you from Sakura. It's going to change everything."

Mack sat a little taller. "So you found it?"

"It's a *magatama* necklace," Fiona explained. "An ancient protection artifact. With it you won't have to worry about what happened at Wyndemere ever happening again. It'll protect you."

Darren handed the talisman to his friend, and Mack's face lit up. He ran his fingers over the ancient jade gemstone. "This is pretty cool," Mack said with a smile.

"Put it on," Gabriella urged.

Mack slid the *magatama* necklace over his head just as his grandfather came into the room. They locked eyes and smiled at each other for the first time since Mack had come back from Wyndemere.

"You look like yourself again," Fiona said.

Darren was watching Fiona when he saw her happy expression suddenly dimmed by confusion and concern.

"Is that supposed to happen?" she asked.

Darren turned back to Mack. The *magatama* had

begun to glow. It looked like it was getting hotter and hotter.

Mack grabbed at it and then pulled his hands away. "It's burning!"

Chapter 8
Remember

Mack looked down to see that the *magatama* pulsed with light as it got hotter and hotter. His heart hammered so hard in his chest that he couldn't catch his breath. The talisman that was supposed to protect him was burning him instead.

He tried to yank it off his neck, but it was too hot to touch.

"Jiichan, help me!" he yelled.

Jiichan looked just as scared as Mack felt, but he came toward him anyway, reaching for the necklace.

Before Jiichan could touch it, and just when Mack thought he couldn't stand the intense burning sensation for one more second, the *magatama* turned bright, fiery red. And then it shattered into a million pieces.

The shocked, scared look on Jiichan's face mirrored his friends' expressions. It scared Mack more than anything.

They look like they're afraid of me, Mack thought.

Jiichan, instead of saying something to make Mack feel better, positioned himself between Mack and his friends.

He thinks he needs to protect them from me, Mack thought.

Anger flared inside him, and Mack took a deep breath to try to calm himself down. It didn't work. Instead, a blinding flash of rage overtook him. It was almost the same feeling he experienced when he was about to attack Gabriella—like it was him or them. Only this time the feeling was ten times stronger.

If I let go and lose control now, he thought, *I may never be able to stop myself again.*

He took another deep breath. Gabriella stepped in front of his grandfather to show him that she wasn't afraid.

"Slowly, Mack," she said, breathing with him. "In . . . and . . . out . . . In . . . and . . . out. Let your thoughts go."

Soon, they were all breathing together, and Mack noticed that his grandfather had visibly relaxed. He was no longer guarding Mack's friends from him, but Mack couldn't help but see that a wary concern was still etched on his face—on all their faces.

His rage flared again. "Will you stop looking at me like that!" he shouted, turning away from them. He began to gather the shards of the *magatama* off the floor, but he couldn't stop ranting. "It's bad enough that I'm stuck at home while you're out on missions, having adventures together and visiting *my* ancestors' homeland," he said. "I know there's something wrong with me, okay? But it's still not fair. Do you have any idea what it's like to know that your best friends are afraid of you?"

Fiona moved toward him, always the first one to try to make anyone feel better, but he didn't want to hear her silly words of optimism right now. He shut her down with a fierce glare.

"You're afraid of me. I can tell. And I know the First Four are trying to fix me, but what if I can't be fixed?

Did you ever think of that? Maybe I'm stuck like this forever, and all of your flying around in the wind won't solve a thing. I'm broken, just like this stupid, useless necklace." He threw the shards he had gathered back to the floor.

"Makoto," Jiichan said. "You mustn't give up."

"Mustn't I?" Mack spat. "You said this talisman would be a magical protection. That it might even cure me. But it didn't, did it? It tried to hurt me instead. If your stupid ancient protection charm can't keep me safe, then probably nothing can."

Mack took a step back. His rage had burned itself out, and he was left feeling helpless and scared. He turned away so his friends wouldn't see that he was blinking back tears.

Jiichan was at his side before he knew it and wrapped his arms around him. Mack buried his head on his grandfather's shoulder and let the tears come. He had worked too hard to control his anger. He had nothing left to battle his tears. At the same time, he hated himself for being weak enough to cry in front of his friends.

His grandfather didn't let go until Mack's tears were

spent. Mack was a little embarrassed, but he felt better, too, as if his tears had carried away a load of worry.

"I'm sorry," he said quietly.

Darren stepped forward and put his hand on Mack's shoulder. "Don't be sorry. I've been feeling scared too," Darren admitted. "This afternoon, it was like, one minute I was a normal kid, having fun at the movies with my friends. The next thing I knew, Sakura's goons were after me."

"You don't have to bottle everything up. Not with us," Fiona said. "Holding it in only makes it worse."

"Yeah, we're the only ones in the world who can relate to what you're feeling," Darren said. "Talk to us. We're here for you."

"Always," Gabriella said. "We're not giving up on you. Don't you give up on us."

"I don't know what's wrong with me," Mack said with a shake of his head. "I've been angry at everyone and everything. Sakura messed with my mind, and the worst part is that I don't know which memories I can trust anymore."

"I have an idea," Gabriella said, checking her watch.

"I have about two hours before curfew, and battling Changers in ancient tunnels is hungry work. What if we order a pizza and hang out? We can tell stories about what we remember from the last year. Then you'll have our memories, too."

Mack smiled slightly. "That's a great idea," he said. "Jiichan?"

His grandfather grinned and lifted the phone from the receiver. "Two extra-large pizzas?" he said.

"With anchovies?" Gabriella asked, her eyes dancing with mischief.

"Ew, gross!" Mack answered with a laugh.

"Okay, okay," Gabriella said, raising her hands in surrender. "No anchovies."

For the next two hours, the group hung out in Mack's room together, munching on pizza with extra cheese and joking around.

"I do remember dreaming I was a fox the night before school started," Mack said. "It was so weird when I looked into the Changing Stone the next day and saw that I *was* one!"

"Do you remembering running into me in the office

the first day of school?" Fiona asked. "You were trying to change your gym class."

"You're right!" Mack said. "I thought an independent study in that musty old gym must have been a mistake."

Fiona smiled. "I'm glad it wasn't."

Mack took in all three of his Changer friends. "I'm glad too," he said.

"Me, three," Darren said. "Even though I was totally freaked out at first."

Gabriella shook her head. "I hid in the bathroom on the first day of school because my eyes had turned yellow, but then they went back to normal. I thought I was going crazy."

"I'm still not sure you *aren't* crazy," Darren said with a laugh. Gabriella punched him in the arm. "Hey! No superstrength at the dinner table."

Gabriella grinned. "Even after I found out what was going on, I kept ruining soccer balls with my claws. I'd be running down the field and all of a sudden, I could feel myself beginning to Change. I was terrified that someone would notice my eyes had turned yellow or that my fingernails and toenails had suddenly become claws."

"But no one ever did?" Mack asked.

Gabriella shook her head. "Trisha said something about my yellow eyes in practice one day, but I told her it must've been a trick of the sun. Thank goodness Ms. Therian and my aunt were able to teach me how to control my transformations."

"Before I learned how to control my powers, I was sending electrical sparks all over the place. I high-fived a kid in the hall once, and his hair floated up from all the static electricity," Darren said.

Mack cracked up. "The same thing happened to Fiona on the first day of school!"

"No way," Darren said.

Fiona took another swig of her soda and nodded. "It's true! You bumped into me on your way to homeroom, then this jerk"—Fiona nudged Mack—"made a terrible pun about my hair."

Gabriella smiled widely. "I need to hear this."

Mack stopped midbite. "I told her the experience was *hair-raising*." At that, the room burst into laughter.

Mack looked around at everyone's smiling faces. How could he ever think that they weren't his friends?

They had never let him down before, and tonight, they'd risked their lives to find a way to save him. Gabriella was right. He wouldn't give up hope.

"Do you remember battling Auden Ironbound on the beach?" Gabriella asked Mack as the room grew quiet again. "You were so brave. The rest of us could only do our best to break the army's focus, but you battled Auden Ironbound one-on-one. And you *beat* him," she added.

Mack smiled. "I earned my second tail that day. I couldn't have done it without all of you. We were a great team," he said.

"We *are* a great team," Darren corrected him.

By the time everyone left, Mack was feeling less alone and less hopeless. He climbed into bed, ready to call it a day.

Jiichan came in to say good night.

"I feel a lot calmer than I did before," Mack said. "Being with my friends helped."

"Hold on to that light, Makoto," his grandfather said. "The warmth you feel from your friends can carry you through any trial. The four of you share a very special bond. Remember that. Nothing can break it."

As Jiichan turned off the light and closed his door, Mack stared into the darkness, hoping his grandfather was right.

Mack woke up the next morning feeling tired. He'd had bad dreams, but he couldn't quite remember what they were about. He knew he was fighting something, and that the fight left him exhausted, but no matter how hard he tried, he couldn't fall back to sleep.

Worse still, he was struggling again to hold on to the happy memories of his friends. He'd felt so sure of their bond just the evening before, but at some point in the night, he'd lost some of that confidence.

When he came out to the kitchen, Mack found a note from Jiichan saying that he'd gone to the store and would be back soon. With nothing else to do, Mack pulled on some jeans and a T-shirt and sat outside, alone on the doorstep, sketching in his notebook.

"Mack!" a familiar voice shouted from across the yard.

"Hey, Joel," Mack said, reluctantly setting his notebook aside. Joel had been Mack's best friend since they were little—until this year, they'd had every class together since kindergarten. Before Mack found out he was a Changer, he'd shared everything with Joel, including a love of comic books and superheroes. "What are you doing here?"

"I've been meaning to give these to you, but I keep forgetting them," Joel said, digging around in his backpack. He finally produced what he was looking for: a set of Agent Underworld comics in Spanish.

Mack's attitude soured instantly. *That's right. While I was busy getting my brain sucked out by the Shadow Fox, you were touring Spain with your parents.*

"Dude?" Joel asked, his hand still extended with the comics.

Mack accepted them and set them on top of his notebook, trying to rein in his anger. *Stop it,* came a small voice inside him. *Joel is your friend. He brought you these because he cares about you.*

"So . . . how was the park trip?" Joel asked, settling in beside Mack on the step. "Did you bring me back a souvenir, maybe that pinecone I asked for?"

Any attempt Mack had at control evaporated in an

instant. He looked at his friend with new eyes as something deep inside himself seemed to take over.

Is he seriously making fun of me because he went on a cool spring break trip and I *didn't? He doesn't even know how many times I've saved his life—saved everyone's life in this stupid town. He's weak. Pathetic. Ungrateful.* I *could swat him aside like a fly right now if* I *wanted to.*

Mack abruptly picked up the comic books and threw them in the mud. Then he grabbed his notebook, turned, and went inside, slamming the door behind him. As Mack walked hurriedly away toward his bedroom, he heard Joel's frantic shouting outside.

"Mack, I'm sorry! I didn't mean to make you mad. I was just joking!"

Mack stopped in his tracks. The small voice came to him again, *This isn't you. This is Sakura.*

Mack fought with himself for several minutes, but he couldn't seem to move. It was as though the part of him that wanted to apologize to Joel was fighting the part of him that wanted to sulk in his room. Finally, he got ahold of himself, darted back to the door, and pulled it open wide.

"Joel, I'm sor—"

But the doorstep was empty. Joel had gone.

Mack was blinded by rage. He slammed the door and knocked one of his grandfather's prized bonsai to the floor. Its porcelain pot shattered on the hardwood floor, reminding him suddenly of the *magatama.*

Attempting to regain control of his anger, Mack tried to do what his grandfather told him and focus on the light he felt inside when he was with his friends. But his mind kept drifting back to the loneliness he felt. And then he thought about how scared—scared of him—everyone had been when the *magatama* shattered. How scared Joel had looked when Mack flung his comic books into the mud.

Mack felt the anger and fear starting to taint his happy memories. One by one, they turned to ash.

Where was Joel or Gabriella or Darren or Fiona when I confronted Sakura? They let me go after her on my own. They weren't there for me when I needed them. They don't really care about me.

His grandfather had warned him against thinking about Sakura, but Mack couldn't help it. His mind drifted back to the forbidden tower at Wyndemere Academy, as if it were a scab he couldn't stop picking at.

I *can't trust Jiichan or the others to help me.* I *need to remember what Sakura said.* Then *maybe* I'll *know what to do.*

Chapter 9
The Jade Jaguar

Across town, Gabriella's grandmother shook Gabriella awake. The night before, Gabriella had filled her *abuelita* in on their successful mission to Japan, followed by the disaster when Mack put on the *magatama.*

"Mack seemed better when we left," Gabriella had said. "But he's sad and scared. I'm worried about him."

"I'll talk to the First Four about next steps," Abuelita had said. "Your aunt will be here tomorrow to help with your training. Try not to worry about it now. Get a good night's sleep."

Gabriella didn't think sleep would come. But it must have been the stress of the battle in Japan or something, because she conked out and slept a deep, dreamless sleep. Now her grandmother was shaking her awake at a time that seemed much too early.

"Wake up, *niña*," Abuelita sang, opening the curtains.

Gabriella opened one eye and then turned over with a groan. She buried her head under the pillow to block out the light and the noise.

Her grandmother shook her again. The sweet, gentle voice was gone. "Up," she barked, sounding like a drill sergeant. "We have work to do."

Work? Gabriella thought. *It's Sunday.*

The events of the night before started to come back to her. The battle in Japan. The *magatama* attacking Mack.

She sat up, and her grandmother handed her a cup of *xocolatl*, the spicy hot chocolate the family turned to on rainy afternoons and bad days.

"Mmm," Gabriella hummed, breathing in its spicy sweetness. "Mom doesn't usually let us have chocolate in the mornings."

"It's our secret. She and Maritza went to New Brighton for a concert," Abuelita said. "Besides, you need the energy. I talked to the First Four last night, and after what happened with the *magatama*, we think it's best that we speed up your training. You're going to have to learn a lot, and quickly."

Gabriella remembered the stricken look on Mack's face last night when the necklace attacked him. *Quickly is right*, she thought. *What if* I *can't learn enough in time to help break Sakura's hold on him?*

Instead of confessing her doubts, she sipped her hot chocolate. The smell of the chili peppers tickled her nose, and the cobwebs of sleep began to dissipate. "I practiced my meditation a lot this week," she said. "I think I have that part down. Pulling back when I start to feel like I might become one with the energy feels natural to me now. I even used the deep, meditative breathing with Mack last night to help him calm down. I think it helped him. I think it helped everybody."

"That's wonderful, *mija*," Abuelita said, kissing her on the forehead. "You're a natural leader, and you've made good progress. Now it's time for the next lesson. Once you're in that meditative state, you can spirit-walk in other people's minds, but you need to learn how to form defenses to use when you're there."

"Defenses against what?" Gabriella asked. "I know I can risk losing my own spirit if I let go and forget myself. What else could happen?"

Her grandmother nodded seriously. "Mack's mind could try to hurt you."

"When I was in Darren's thoughts nothing attacked me. He just kept wandering into different dreams and memories. I didn't feel like I was in danger."

"Most people aren't capable of defending their minds without practice, but Sakura has powerful, dark magic. And she's smart. Before she went rogue she was trained by the best: Akira Kimura. She'll be expecting someone to spirit-walk in Mack's mind, to try to help him, and she may have planted different things in his head that you'll need to find your way around."

"Like what?"

"It may be as simple as defensive strategies that could push you out of Mack's thoughts before you can really see what's happening in there," Abuelita said. "But it could be more than that, too. Sakura might have planted magic that will automatically attack any intruder it detects."

Gabriella no longer needed the *xocolatl* to wipe the sleep way. She was wide-awake. "What would those attacks do?" Gabriella asked.

"We really don't know," Abuelita admitted. She closed her eyes and sighed. "I hate that we're putting you in so much danger."

Gabriella shook her head. "If I don't do this, we're in even bigger danger, aren't we? Sakura is seriously evil."

"She is," Abuelita said, "but good outstrips evil every time—at least in the long run. And your *tía* and I are going to make sure you're ready for whatever comes."

Gabriella took a last sip of her *xocolatl* and put down the cup. "Let's get started."

Together, they headed into the guest room where Abuelita was staying during her monthlong visit. A minute later, Tía Rosa knocked on the door.

"Are you ready to tiptoe through my thoughts and dreams?" Tía Rosa asked with a smile.

"Wait . . . I'm practicing on *you*?" Gabriella asked.

"I'll try to think good thoughts," her aunt joked, "but you're going to have to work for them."

"Think about what you're going to give me for my birthday," Gabriella joked. "That way I can get a sneak peek."

Tía Rosa was about to respond when Abuelita clapped her hands. "Come, let's get serious," she said. "There's no time to lose. You'll enter Rosa's mind, and she'll put up defenses for you to try to work around. She will even attack you."

Gabriella got serious too. "Really?"

I *know* Tía Rosa *won't hurt me, but there's so much that could go wrong,* she thought.

"I'll be at your side, helping," her grandmother said. "We'll do it together. Are you ready?"

"Ready," Gabriella answered.

Both she and her grandmother began to meditate. Soon, Gabriella could feel the two of them breathing in unison. Then her grandmother took Gabriella's hand. They left their bodies and willed themselves into Tía Rosa's mind. Gabriella glanced back at her body, still breathing in unison with her grandmother's. I *will never get used to seeing that,* she thought before she fell into her aunt's thoughts.

She saw her aunt letting herself into the house that morning.

It's not as strange as it was when I stepped into Darren's mind, Gabriella thought. *It's becoming more natural to me. Oh no—*

Before she had even finished the thought, Gabriella was pushed out of her aunt's mind.

"Try not to stay so rooted in your own thoughts," Abuelita said after they both came out of their meditative states. "You want to know what Tía Rosa is thinking and feeling."

"Okay," Gabriella said with a nod. "Let's try again."

She and Abuelita started to breathe together once more, and—faster this time—they willed themselves into Tía Rosa's mind. For a moment, Gabriella felt fuzzy, as if she were asleep and about to enter her own dream. Then her grandmother broke through the mist.

"Stay with me, Gabriella," she said.

"I'm here," Gabriella answered. She could see that both she and her grandmother had taken their *nahual* forms.

The mist swirled, and they were again in Tía Rosa's

mind. This time Gabriella saw flashes of images—Tía Rosa driving along the coast from New Brighton to Willow Cove, pulling into the driveway, and opening the front door. Then Abuelita got her attention again. As Gabriella watched, her grandmother transformed from a *nahual* into a fluffy kitten and then into her human form.

"You can hide your appearance," Abuelita explained. "You don't always have to take your jaguar form. That way you can hide in your target's mind."

"Hide?" Gabriella asked.

"If you seem like you're simply a part of a memory, or a dream, it'll be easier for you to slip by a person's mental defenses. Someone who would put up a fight against a jaguar, for instance, wouldn't worry about a kitten or someone they know well."

Before Gabriella had a chance to try to transform, Tía Rosa's mind had moved on to a family barbecue just before school started last summer. She didn't notice Abuelita, who had taken her human form and fit nicely into the scene. Rosa was putting paper plates, napkins, and utensils on a picnic table. But she saw Gabriella in her jaguar form and used a mind defense technique to push her niece out of the memory.

Gabriella tried to push back, to stay in her aunt's mind, but the effort woke her up from the meditation. She was back in her house, blinking at the sunlight coming through the window.

Tía Rosa smiled at her. "Now you know why it takes most of us years to master spirit-walking," she said. "But that was a good effort. You tried to push back, which is exactly what you are supposed to do. If you were in your human form, I might not have noticed you at all."

"Let's try again," Abuelita said. "It's natural for you to take your *nahual* form when you spirit-walk, but try to transform the minute we enter Rosa's mind."

"Is it different from transforming when I'm in my actual body?" Gabriella asked.

"It's just like transforming when you're not spirit-walking. You think about it, and then it happens. At first it's difficult—it takes concentration and determination—but it soon begins to feel like it usually does," her grandmother answered.

"Okay," Gabriella said. "I'll try."

Once again she and her grandmother entered their meditative states. Then they willed themselves into Tía Rosa's mind.

This time Gabriella found herself in what looked more like a dream than a memory. Her aunt was running down the street dressed like the Emerald Wildcat. Shortly after Gabriella learned she was a Changer, she had stumbled across her aunt's crime-fighting mask in the attic. Dressed in black and wearing an emerald-green mask, her aunt had used her *nahual* powers to fight crime and bring justice, just like a real superhero! Gabriella had discovered that many of her own *nahual* powers, like her aunt's, were available to her in her human form—especially on the soccer field.

Still in her *nahual* form, Gabriella kept to the edges of the memory. She watched her aunt chase down a purse thief. The memory was so exciting that Gabriella forgot to try to transform her appearance until she saw Abuelita, in her human form, standing on the sidelines and cheering with the onlookers.

Gabriella concentrated hard, willing a change into her human self. The next thing she knew she had transformed into the Jade Jaguar, the sidekick she had dreamed up for the Emerald Wildcat in a homemade comic book.

"Nice threads, *mija*," her aunt said as they left the street and scaled a building.

"Thanks!" Gabriella leaped across rooftops on her aunt's heels, still in pursuit of the purse thief.

The thief reached the edge of a rooftop. The distance between that and the next one was too far for him to jump, not without falling to the street below. He turned on them, ready to fight.

Gabriella had to focus again and bring her *nahual* powers to battle the thief, but this dream—just like a real one—took strange twists and turns. The purse thief morphed into Abuelita. Now Gabriella's grandmother was trying to push her out of the dream.

This time, Gabriella pushed back. *Nobody messes with the Jade Jaguar. Mack taught me everything I know about superheroes. He showed me how to create a hero who's strong and daring, unbeatable in a fight. And now I'm going to be the hero who saves him.*

"Well done, *mija*," her grandmother said. Then she

signaled that it was time to leave Tía Rosa's mind.

Gabriella had almost forgotten that she was really in the guest room. "You talked to me when I was running with you," she said to her aunt. "Did you know it was me? Or did you think it was part of your daydream?"

"I knew it was you and not a memory, but only because I knew to look for you," Tía Rosa answered. "You were so convincing that in a normal dream, I would have thought you were just another dream element. Abuelita was right. Well done, *mija*."

Gabriella felt exhausted and exhilarated at the same time. Transforming inside her aunt's mind was harder than she thought it would be, and standing her ground against that last push took every bit of energy she had.

"That push is part of an ancient set of skills known to spirit warriors," Abuelita explained. "Some of us have mastered fighting skills using only our spiritual energy. You'll learn to draw on your feelings—your love for your friends, for example—to fight. Just let the power of the emotion surge through you. It will give you a strength you didn't know you had."

"I was thinking of the comic I created with Mack's

help when you tried to push me out of Tía Rosa's mind. And then I thought about how I was doing this to help him," Gabriella explained.

"Remember that feeling," Abuelita said. "You were strong and determined. That will see you through."

"As a spirit warrior your *nahual* powers can be multiplied as long as your spirit remains strong and unbroken," Tía Rosa said. "That's the strength that will allow you to save your friend. To battle against whatever evil Sakura has planted in his mind."

"Don't ever doubt the good and true emotions, like love and friendship, that are driving your spirit," her grandmother added. "Doubts will cause your power to crumble, and then you won't be able to help anyone, not even yourself."

Gabriella nodded. She was feeling stronger than ever. Looking down at her hands, she felt a rush of reassurance in spite of the dangers. I *am a spirit warrior like my grandmother and aunt before me*, Gabriella thought. *And I'm going to save my friend.*

Chapter 10
Una

On Monday afternoon, Fiona ran down the hall to Changer class. Mack, Darren, and Gabriella were already training when she arrived. Mack was aiming fireballs at a moving target while Darren practiced creating stronger and stronger force fields. Gabriella moved through an agility course, slipping through it on quiet paws, twisting and turning to avoid obstacles that leaped out of nowhere.

"Sorry, Ms. Therian," Fiona called, giving everyone a small wave. "I got held up."

Ms. Therian walked over to Fiona and said, "What did you and your mother work on over the weekend?"

"The tide song again," Fiona told her. "I think I've got it down now. At first I couldn't control the size of the waves, but now I know how to modulate my voice so that I can make the waves big or small or even gigantic—whatever I might need."

"Very good," Ms. Therian said. "Work on that some more in the pool today."

Fiona was a little disappointed—she could only sing *selkie* songs in her human form. While she was grateful to have finally learned a few (they were, after all, her only defense against land-based attacks), she loved every minute in her *selkie* form and would have gladly just swam in the pool for the entire period.

"I need to step out for a minute," Ms. Therian told them. "Keep on with what you're doing. You all look great."

Fiona turned back to the pool. She had to concentrate harder and sing for a longer period of time than she did in the ocean before her waves began to form. *Selkie* songs relied on the natural ebb and flow of the ocean waves and the tides. A pool doesn't naturally have tides or waves, so she had to work harder to achieve results. And those results weren't nearly as spectacular.

Because the pool was a lot smaller than the ocean, before Fiona realized it, her waves were bigger than she expected. The next thing she knew, one had burst free from the pool and came crashing down on Mack and his fire bow.

Mack transformed from a drenched *kitsune* to a drenched boy in the blink of an eye. Steam rose from his feet and hands where there had been fire a moment before.

Fiona laughed playfully. "Sorry, I—"

Mack turned to her, his face pinched and angry. "What do you think you're doing?" he demanded.

"I'm sorry. It was a mistake," she said. "This is only my second time singing the tide song in the pool. It's so different from in the ocean. I didn't mean—"

"'I *didn't mean*,'" Mack imitated in a high-pitched girlie voice. "Get some control."

"Dude, it was an honest mistake," Darren said, walking over.

"Yeah, she didn't mean it," Gabriella added.

"Oh great; now you're all ganging up on me," Mack

said. "And when you're not ganging up on me, you're leaving me out."

Fiona tried to explain again. "Mack, that's not—"

"Cut it, Fiona, I don't care what you have to say." Mack stepped back and surveyed the three of them. "I am so sick of being your punching bag." He stomped over to the bleachers and grabbed his backpack. "Things are going to change, and soon. I hope you're ready." Then he threw the backpack over his shoulder and stormed out of the gym, passing Ms. Therian on the way.

"Mack, what happened?" she asked.

"Ask them," he snapped.

Fiona watched the doors swing shut behind him. "I don't know why he got so angry," she said. "I got him wet by accident, and he was furious."

"We tried to calm him down," Darren added, "but that just made everything worse. He accused us of ganging up on him."

"I'm sorry," Fiona said, blinking back tears. "It really was an accident."

"It's not your fault, Fiona," Ms. Therian said. "Mack's on edge right now. If it wasn't your wave, something else would have set him off. You can't blame yourself."

The bell rang to signal the end of the school day.

"Go on and catch your buses," Ms. Therian said. "I'll let Mack's grandfather know what happened. We can talk about it tomorrow after he's calmed down."

Fiona didn't want to leave things until tomorrow. She hated to think that Mack believed she got him wet on purpose. And his idea that they were all using him as a punching bag was even worse.

Does he really believe that? Or was he just yelling to let off steam?

Fiona decided she had to find him and apologize again—and get him to see that she didn't mean any harm—before they left school. She searched for him in the tide of students rushing for their buses, but didn't see him anywhere. She ran down to the room where the comic book club met after school, but he wasn't there either, and no one had seen him.

Finally, she realized she was about to miss her own ride home and gave up. She got to the bus just as the driver was about to close the doors.

I'll call Mack later. Maybe he'll be feeling better then.

As usual Fiona sat by herself in the front seat behind the driver. Normally, she used this time to get a head start on her homework, but today, she could only think about Mack.

He's getting worse. A month ago Mack would have cracked up if I *drenched him with a wave. He'd make some kind of joke and threaten to evaporate the pool with his fire arrows.*

Fiona got all the way home without writing even one sentence of her Celtic mythology report. She got off the bus and noticed that the driveway was empty. Her father wasn't home yet, so she dug her keys out of her backpack and let herself in the front door.

I *guess* I'll *go see if there's anything to cook for dinner*, she thought. I *know* Dad *won't want spaghetti surprise again.*

Fiona was humming to herself when she entered the kitchen, but stopped short when she saw someone sitting at the kitchen table. She dashed back to the front hall and pulled her cell phone from the front pocket of her backpack.

"I'm calling the police!" she yelled, reaching for the front door.

"Please don't," the woman said, coming out of the kitchen. "I just want to talk."

Fiona's back was pressed up against the door. She had one hand on the doorknob behind her. In the other she held her phone. She pressed the 9 and then the 1. She was about to dial the third number when the woman stepped into the light. She was drenched from head to toe, wearing a simple cotton dress that was discolored and sandy at the edges. Seaweed was tangled in her long, braided hair.

"Please," the woman pleaded. "I'm sorry for barging in, but it's been a long time since I've had to do human things."

It suddenly came back to Fiona—with her mother's enchantments in place, the only magical beings who could enter the house were *selkies*. As the woman took one more step into the light, Fiona saw her face and recognized the woman. It was Una, one of her mother's attendants. They'd spoken a few times over the past months, but something about Una was different now. There was a look of desperation in her eyes, and her hands were trembling.

Fiona had calmed down for a moment, but then her heart quickened again. "What are you doing here? Did my mother send you? Is she all right?" Fiona asked.

"It's Sakura," Una said breathlessly. "She's here, in Willow Cove. She has your mother."

Fiona gasped. "But how?"

"I don't know, but she wants our support in exchange for Leana. The *selkie* council has ruled that only you can conduct the negotiations to get her back," Una said. "We need you; you're the only other *selkie* of royal blood."

Fiona remembered her mother telling her that Sakura wanted the *selkies* to join her in her war against the Changers, but even so, Fiona felt suspicious. The council didn't take Fiona at all seriously when she met with them at her mother's side a few months ago. In fact, when Fiona suggested they unite with the Changer nation to battle Auden Ironbound together, they had laughed at her. They brushed off her concerns as those of a naive youngling.

Why would they suddenly trust and respect me enough to want my help now?

Almost before Fiona had fully formed that thought, it was drowned out by her fear—no, terror—at the idea of losing her mother. They had been separated for nine years when the *selkies* split off from the Changer nation. Things had been so bad that Fiona's mother thought it necessary for Fiona to believe that she was dead to protect her.

No, I *can't lose my mother again.* I *only just found her.* I'll *face whatever* I *have to, even the Shadow* Fox, *to see her again.*

"Take me to them," Fiona said, digging her *selkie* cloak out of her backpack and fastening it around her neck.

"Follow me," Una said. "And hurry. We've no time to lose."

Fiona did as she was told. Fiona's heart was beating much too fast, but she reminded herself that the First Four had assigned guards to her and to the others.

They're watching me, Fiona told herself. *They'll step in to protect me if* I *need help. Just like they did for* Darren.

Una led her out onto the street and beyond the range of her mother's protection spell. She felt a change in the air as she stepped over the protective boundary. The street and the small patch of woods across the street were free from enchantments.

How quickly can I *get to the protected area on the beach if* I *need to?* Fiona wondered.

Una was moving farther away from those protections. She was getting more and more agitated, telling Fiona to hurry. At one point she grabbed Fiona's hand to force her to move faster.

A man and woman suddenly appeared on the street, stepping out from behind a tree. Una shoved Fiona toward them. The woman grabbed Fiona roughly by the shoulders, her fingernails digging in like sharp talons. Her eyes were strange and glittery.

"I've done what you asked. Now give me my cloak back," Una demanded.

The man only smirked at her.

Una's voice rose into a frantic scream. "You said the girl for the cloak!"

They've got her selkie *cloak,* Fiona realized. *The worst thing that can ever happen to a* selkie *is to lose her cloak. To be trapped in her human body forever. How could she have been so careless?*

The man laughed and threw Una her cloak. She grabbed it and tucked the cloak tightly under her arm. "I'm sorry. My magic isn't powerful enough to fight them. They threatened to burn my cloak if I didn't do what they said," she whispered to Fiona before she turned around and ran toward the stairs that led from the cliff to the sea.

You should have asked my mother for help, Fiona thought, *instead of turning on us.*

But Fiona didn't speak. She was quietly singing the tide song under her breath. *Selkie* songs couldn't be rushed. They had to be sung to the rhythm of the waves and the tides. Still, she sang this one as if she was in a choppy, storm-filled, fast-moving sea. She saw the waves getting bigger and more agitated.

The woman was about to clap Fiona's wrists and ankles in magical chains when she saw a wave—larger than anything Fiona had ever created before—rear up out of the sea. The woman's mouth twisted with hatred. "Stop singing," she demanded. "Or it will be your last."

She wouldn't dare, Fiona told herself. *They're trying to get to my mother through me. Sakura wants the* selkies *on her side. Harming me would make sure that never happens.* She kept singing. The wave ebbed and then flowed again—bigger now.

In a flash, the man transformed into a *nykur,* his

horse hooves raking the ground impatiently. The woman dug her nails into Fiona's shoulders and dragged her onto the horse's back as he set off at a gallop.

But he couldn't outrun her wave. It loomed over them like a wall of water. The top of the swell curled over their heads, and there was a moment of hesitation. Fiona smiled. There was no way a *nykur* and whatever kind of Changer this woman was could outswim a *selkie*. She sang the last note and transformed just as the tidal wave crashed down on them with a roar, carrying both Changers away. Fiona flicked her tail to get away from them and swam to the top of the whitecaps. As soon as they dispersed, she transformed again, got to her feet, and ran back to the protection of the house.

Her cell phone forgotten, Fiona ran for the land-line in the front hall and dialed the first number she could think of: Gabriella's. At the same time she double-checked that all the doors in the house were locked.

"Sakura's forces tried to kidnap me," she said when Gabriella finally answered. "My guards weren't here to help," Fiona said frantically. "I don't know what to do!"

"What happened?" Gabriella asked.

Fiona told the story as quickly as she could. "My guards weren't here," she repeated. "Sakura's people may have gotten to them first!"

Fiona heard Gabriella sharing the story with her grandmother.

"Tía Rosa is already on her way," Gabriella said. "I'm putting my grandmother on the phone."

"Are they still there, Fiona?" Gabriella's grandmother asked. "Are you safe?"

"I think I'm safe as long as I don't leave the house. They washed away in my wave, but they could come back." Fiona peeked out the window. "There's an *impundulu* flying overhead—I think it's that woman—and she's creating a storm. Can you come here, please?"

"Yes, of course," Gabriella's grandmother said. "Rosa will be there in seconds. We'll alert the others and be there as soon as we can."

A huge lightning bolt ripped through the sky, aiming for the electrical box on the side of Fiona's house. Her mother's protection field seemed to repel it. But it couldn't repel the bolt that struck the other end of the street, aiming for the power and telephone lines that fed the whole neighborhood.

"Hurry!" Fiona added. But just as she was saying the word, the phone line went dead. Another stroke of lightning sliced through the sky. It was followed by another and another.

Chapter 11
TIME IS UP

Gabriella was just finishing up her latest spirit-walking lesson with her grandmother and her aunt when she received Fiona's desperate phone call. Tía Rosa was on her way to Fiona's house before they had even heard the full story. Gabriella and her grandmother hopped into the car to go to the Kimuras' house.

On the way, Gabriella tried to communicate telepathically with Mack, but her attempts were rebuffed. Reaching Mr. Kimura was harder; for some reason his mind was closed. She wasn't able to get through to him.

When they got to the house, she raced up the front walk and pounded on the door.

Please be home, she begged silently.

It seemed to take forever for Mack to answer the door. When he did, and he saw Gabriella, he slammed it in her face.

Startled, Gabriella stepped back for a moment and then started banging on the door again. "Fiona's in trouble," she yelled. "She needs us! Are you seriously going to ignore that because you're mad at us?"

When the door opened again, it was Mr. Kimura who greeted her. Mack stood behind him, smirking.

"Sakura's people tried to take Fiona," Gabriella told him. "She held them off for now, but she needs our help."

Mr. Kimura closed his eyes for a moment, and Gabriella could tell he was communicating telepathically with other Changers. "We must go," he said to Gabriella and Mack. "Darren will join us on the way. Changer forms will be fastest."

Mr. Kimura and Gabriella transformed immediately. Abuelita did the same. Mack rolled his eyes and took his time, but he did finally transform.

Why is he being like this? Gabriella wondered. *It's Fiona!*

Mr. Kimura performed a cloaking illusion so that

they could run through the streets of Willow Cove without attracting the attention of nonmagical people or Sakura's forces. Darren joined them as they raced past his home, transforming so that he could fly above them.

Gabriella was frightened for her friend, but despite her fears and her need to get to Fiona as quickly as possible, Gabriella couldn't help but notice that the fire around Mack's paws looked different. It was darker than the bright oranges and yellows she was accustomed to seeing. And the new deep umber color didn't seem to carry the same heat. She compared it to the bright-white flames that licked at Mr. Kimura's paws.

Something's definitely off, she thought. *Even the way the flame is moving is different. Instead of reaching up and out like normal flames, these are sticking closer to Mack's paws. Has Mr. Kimura noticed?*

There wasn't time to discuss the finer points of *kitsune* fire as they raced through town. Finally, they reached Fiona's house in time to find a massive battle raging on the street and in the small patch of woods that stood between the street and the beach.

Tía Rosa was doing her best to hold off both the *nykur*

and the *impundulu* on her own. Gabriella could see that she was having a difficult time, and she was relieved to see Abuelita and Mr. Kimura join the fight.

Stay back, Mr. Kimura communicated. *Keep yourselves safe.*

Darren and Mack stayed where they were, watching the battle, but Gabriella ran in the direction of Fiona's house. She changed back into her human form.

"I'll check on Fiona!" she shouted over her shoulder, but she was repelled by Fiona's mother's enchantments. She saw nothing in front of her, but she couldn't break through the invisible shield. *Fiona, we're here,* she said telepathically. *We're here to help.*

Moments later, Fiona ran toward Gabriella, holding her *selkie* cloak. She and Gabriella joined Darren and Mack, who had already transformed back into their human forms. They watched the battle while Fiona filled them in on what had happened with Una.

"Wow, Una was ready to turn her back on her queen and just hand you over to Sakura?" Darren asked. "I wouldn't want to be her the next time she faces your mother and the *selkie* council."

"For *selkies*, losing their cloak is the very worst thing that can happen to them," Fiona explained. "Worse than death, even. I feel a little bit sorry for Una, but I don't think my mother will. Una is probably miles away by now." She kept her eyes on the battle. "Wow, Gabriella, your aunt and grandmother are amazing fighters."

"They are," Gabriella agreed. She couldn't help but marvel as she watched her grandmother—yes, her *grandmother*—fight so artfully. In her human form Abuelita looked like a harmless little old lady who puttered around in the kitchen and complained about sore knees. In her *nahual* form there was nothing grandmotherly or old about her. Her spotted jaguar pelt shined as she launched a new series of attacks.

She's so sleek and powerful.

Gabriella watched Abuelita launch her body into the air and deflect the *nykur* with her sharp claws. When he stumbled backward, she narrowed her yellow eyes, and a burst of white energy pushed the enemies back.

She said nahuals *can use spiritual powers to fight. Is that what she's doing now?*

The *nykur* seemed to lose control of his legs. Then

he came down hard on them. Gabriella heard a crack and thought at least one leg must be broken. Before she could find out, the *impundulu*, who had been shooting lightning bolts toward them this whole time, swooped down right toward her *abuelita*.

"Watch out!" Gabriella yelled.

Mr. Kimura and Tía Rosa jumped between Abuelita and the *impundulu*, pushing the lightning bird away.

Gabriella wanted to cheer for them all, but she was horribly frightened at the same time. She turned to the others to say, "Do you think they'll be all right?" But before she could get the words out, she realized that something was happening to Mack. Something very, very strange.

Mack was watching the battle rage on, and he was laughing.

It wasn't an ordinary laugh. It was terrifying. Mack watched his grandfather struggle with the *impundulu*, and he was enjoying himself.

He's delusional, Gabriella thought. She transformed back, ready for action.

Then she noticed that Mack's eyes had turned jet-black. They were all pupils, with no iris at all. And there were black flames hovering around his hands.

"Mack!" Gabriella said. "What's going on?"

He laughed harder and sent a fireball in her direction. Gabriella had to duck to avoid it.

"What is wrong with you?" Darren shouted. He grabbed Mack's arms and tried to hold him still, but Mack shook him off like he was nothing.

"I . . . don't . . . know!" Mack shouted in between waves of frenzied laughter. He clutched his stomach. Sooty flames enveloped his arms. "I . . . can't . . . stop!"

Gabriella thought he might throw another fireball, this time at Darren. She changed into her *nahual* form and pinned Mack to the ground, but he threw her off with a burst of flame.

Mack transformed. He and Gabriella circled each other, both ready to launch into battle.

What is happening? Gabriella thought. I *don't want to fight Mack.*

Suddenly, they were joined by the adults. Only then did Gabriella realize that the *nykur* and *impundulu* had retreated. She wouldn't be surprised if they went to get reinforcements.

We have to stop whatever this is before they come back with more of Sakura's fighters, she thought. *We can't battle Mack and them at the same time.*

Mr. Kimura, now in his human form, jumped between Mack and Gabriella and knocked his grandson out with a flick of his wrist. In a flash, he caught Mack gently in his arms and laid him on the ground. As he fell, Mack became human again. So did Gabriella.

"He's unconscious," Mr. Kimura said.

Mack's breathing was fast and uneven. He seemed to be struggling against something. Gabriella saw pain and fear on his face.

"Sakura is taking hold of him," Mr. Kimura said, his voice anguished. He stroked the side of Mack's face. "He doesn't have a lot of time left before her dark magic takes over him completely."

Abuelita took Gabriella's hands in hers. "It's now or never, *mija*," she said.

"Are you sure you're ready?" Mr. Kimura asked her.

Gabriella took a deep breath. "I'm as ready as I can be." She twirled the Ring of Tezcatlipoca on her finger.

"Darren, we need a force field, in case reinforcements arrive. You'll need to hold it for as long as you can. Do nothing else. Can you do that?" Mr. Kimura asked.

Darren nodded, looking a little confused.

"Gabriella is going to spirit-walk in Mack's mind," Mr. Kimura explained.

Darren raised his hands. His fingertips crackled with electric current. He drew his hands together, and the sparks united, forming a glowing force field. Then he drew an orb in the air, which grew big enough to encircle all of them.

"Where are Sefu and Yara?" Abuelita asked Mr. Kimura. "We'll need them if Sakura's forces return."

"Sefu and Yara are halfway around the world on another mission, but Dorina is amassing backup. They'll be here soon."

Abuelita turned to Gabriella with a nod. "You can do this, *mija*. I know you can."

Safe inside the protective force field, Gabriella sat next to Mack and began to meditate, ignoring his shallow, uneven breaths and focusing on her own. *In . . . and . . . out,* she told herself. *In . . . and . . . out.*

Before she knew it, she was above her body. She could see everything with a spiritual clarity. In her spirit form, she walked over to Mack. *Now or never,* Gabriella thought, and willed herself to enter his mind.

Chapter 12
The Dark Gift

When Gabriella arrived in Mack's thoughts, she first concentrated on transforming into her human self. She thought it would be easy to hide in the shadows of his memories, but Mack's mind was strangely blank. An endless white space stretched out before Gabriella, and she was alone except for Mack and a jet-black Shadow Fox with three tails. Mack was focused so completely on the fox, he wasn't aware of anything else going on—even Gabriella.

Sakura has seven tails, Gabriella remembered. *This can't be Sakura. It's Mack's* kitsune *form. But his fur has turned black, just like hers.*

From the fox, Gabriella could feel a chilling darkness spreading over Mack's mind. It crept into happy memories, infecting them with bitterness and sadness. She watched as pockets of joy were distorted into anger and emptiness. And she could also feel how exhausted Mack was. This three-tailed fox was slowly draining all his energy, leaving him unable to battle against the rage and hopelessness that was taking over. She could tell that Mack was both repulsed by, and drawn to, the darkness. The inky-black fox fed on his fear, and it was getting stronger and stronger.

So this is what was happening to Mack all this time, she realized. *No wonder he doesn't want to struggle against it anymore. All the fight has gone out of him.*

Abuelita had told Gabriella to use her feelings to help her find out what was happening in Mack's mind in order to help him. *Maybe Mack can use my anger to fight Sakura,* she thought.

She let her anger at Sakura course through her veins. She would channel it into spiritual energy to save her friend.

Gabriella's surge of energy attracted Mack's attention.

"Gabriella," he said. "I'm so sorry. The fox . . . It's ruining everything," he said, stumbling over his words. "I didn't mean all those things I said. I've been fighting it so hard. . . ."

Gabriella took a step toward him to take his hand, but the fox was sneaky. It reappeared, as if out of nowhere, and pounced on Gabriella. She was jolted from Mack's mind.

Gabriella opened her eyes and saw that Darren's force field had shrank. She couldn't see Mr. Kimura or the other adults. The four kids were the only ones inside the protective dome, and she could hear the muffled chaos of battle coming from outside. More of Sakura's soldiers had arrived.

Gabriella didn't have time to ask Darren or Fiona what was happening. She closed her eyes again and focused on her breathing. In an instant, she was back in her meditative state, willing herself into Mack's mind.

She saw the three-tailed fox closing in on her friend, its jaws wide-open, showing off rows of sharp teeth. The creature was about to devour him completely.

Gabriella didn't have time to transform or hide. She

needed every bit of energy and concentration to save Mack. She galloped toward the *kitsune* in her *nahual* form and dug her claws into its haunches. She dragged it backward, away from her friend, and heard the fox howl in pain.

Gabriella used the same spirit warrior techniques on the fox that Tía Rosa had taught her. She was using her spiritual energy to push the fox farther and farther from Mack, but the *kitsune* wasn't going down so easily.

Rage coursed through Gabriella. "Get away from him!" she shouted.

The fox retreated, but Gabriella didn't think it was entirely gone. She sensed it was lurking somewhere, regaining strength to fight again.

Gabriella wasn't sure she was strong enough to completely drive it from Mack's mind. It was a part of Mack in a way she could never be. She needed help.

She turned to Mack. *You have to fight it too, Mack!* she yelled.

"I can't," Mack said limply. "It's part of me now. I can't destroy myself."

No! It's not you. It's Sakura. She's planted this thing in your head to infect your memories. Fight it, Mack! You have to fight it!

"I'm trying," Mack said. "I've been trying and trying, ever since Wyndemere. I can't anymore. I'm *so* tired. I just want to go. Let me go."

No! Gabriella shouted. *I won't let you go. You have to help me save you!*

"It's too late. Don't you see? Sakura has won. I'm sorry."

Mack turned away from her, and Gabriella felt the fur on her neck stand up. While she was focused on Mack, the three-tailed fox had quietly reappeared. Before she could react, it attacked her.

She shook it off. She tried to push it away with her spiritual energy, but she didn't have the strength. She was distracted; Mack's desire to give up had scared her, and fear was blocking her powers.

The fox snarled at her, and Gabriella realized it sounded just like Mack's snarl in class last week. She remembered Mack lunging at her, as if she were his enemy.

"I'm sorry," Mack said again. For a moment, it looked

like he mustered all the goodness he could, before he let the Shadow Fox take over. "Tell Jiichan—tell Jiichan I'm sorry."

Then Mack's eyes flashed again.

The last thing Gabriella saw before being pushed out completely was the jaws of the three-tailed *kitsune* as they closed around Mack's leg.

Chapter 13
Sakura's Apprentice

No longer unconscious, Mack rose to his feet and glared at Gabriella. *How dare she mess with my mind,* he thought. He was filled with anger and a kind of hungry power he had never known before. He could feel it burning inside him, ready to consume more and more.

So this is what true power feels like. No *wonder the old man didn't want me to have this.*

He loomed above Gabriella, who was sitting cross-legged on the ground with tears running down her face. "Fight it, Mack!" she yelled. "Fight it!"

"Fight what?" Mack said with a laugh. "My new power? Can't you see that this is me? I'm more powerful than you'll ever be. Than *any* of you will ever be."

He sneered at Darren and Fiona, still hovering over Gabriella. "What a bunch of weaklings you are. I can see you now for what you are: jealous. Pathetic." He swung his arms out and knocked his former friends out of his path with fiery blasts, breathing in the sharp odor of ash that surrounded him now.

Darren's grip on the force field dissolved. The four kids stood in the midst of battle, totally unprotected.

Mack saw his grandfather battling two Changers at once. The old man's head swiveled, and he lost focus when he saw Mack's transformation into a three-tailed shadow fox.

Want to take me on? Mack thought.

But before his grandfather could do or say anything, Sakura arrived on the battlefield.

Everything stopped. Everyone—both his grandfather's cronies and Sakura's warriors—paused to look at her.

That's command, Mack thought. *Even the old man should be paying her respect.*

Awed by her supremacy, by her power, Mack

darted over to her, leaving fiery footsteps in the grass. He Changed to his human form and bowed. "Master," he said. "I am ready to be your student. I await your command."

"Ah, my apprentice. We are reunited at last," Sakura said. She put a hand on Mack's shoulder and faced Mack's grandfather, her old teacher, with a challenge in her eyes.

Mack stood at her side, eyeing his grandfather with the same challenge. "I'm sorry it took me so long to rejoin you," he told Sakura. "The old man held me back, as did they." He waved his arm in the direction of Gabriella, Fiona, and Darren. "It was foolish of them, but I've broken free now. I am ready to begin my studies."

"Together we will take this world," Sakura said. "But there's something I need to attend to first."

She turned and transformed into a seven-tailed jet-black fox in one breath, just in time for Mr. Kimura to rush the two of them in his *kitsune* form. Mack saw that Sakura's forces were now on the ground, unconscious. Ms. Therian stood over them with a satisfied expression, ready to battle Sakura if she was needed.

Sakura and Mack disappeared as his grandfather approached. Then they reappeared behind him. The old man spun on his heel, but then they did the trick again and again.

Mack laughed. "What magic is this?" he asked.

Sakura only smiled at him. Then she turned to her old teacher and communicated telepathically. *You've lost, Akira,* she said. *You once took something from me—and with it, hope, love, my dreams—all in one breath. Forgive me if* I *take this opportunity to return the favor.*

Mack watched his grandfather come at Sakura once again, confident that the old man would fail. Sakura pushed Mack out of the way, and this time she engaged Akira. The two *kitsune* circled each other, one angry and one triumphant. They sparred, dodging each other's flames. In a few minutes, Mack's grandfather—who had already battled and defeated many of Sakura's soldiers that day—was winded.

Mack was impressed by his new master's stamina. By her control. By her dark power. *Sakura will make a far better teacher than my grandfather ever could be,* he thought.

Now, she stood back and smirked at the old man.

We'll continue this another day, Akira. Then she turned to Mack. *Come, my apprentice.*

She transformed back and waved her arm. A dark portal appeared where just a moment before there had been sun and air. The hole sucked the light into it, beckoning to Mack.

Mack took his human form and ran forward.

In a last-ditch effort Darren tried to envelope Mack in a protective force field to keep him from escaping. It worked for a moment, but then Sakura snapped her fingers and shattered his hold on him. Darren suddenly looked unspeakably weak and helpless as Mack bellowed with laughter and then disappeared through the portal, right on Sakura's heels.

EPILOGUE

Suddenly, the street was dead silent. It was as if Sakura had taken everything with her—the sound of the ocean's waves, the birds chirping in the trees, even the soft buzz of insects.

Darren collapsed on the ground, eyes closed, completely spent from his effort to protect his friends with his force fields. He could hear Gabriella's choking sobs from somewhere nearby and the gentle tones of her aunt and grandmother telling her that it wasn't her fault. He wanted to join them, to try to make his friend feel better, but he didn't have the energy.

He saw Mr. Kimura staring into the space where

the hole had been, as if willing it to come back.

"Where did Mack go?" Fiona asked Ms. Therian. "What does this mean?"

"I'm not sure," Ms. Therian answered. "Sakura has many bases of operation; usually by the time the Changer nation finds one, it's been abandoned."

Darren sat up.

Mr. Kimura walked across the street to the cliffside and gazed out over the sea. The sun was setting over the ocean.

Darren usually thought of sunsets as peaceful, but not this one. This sky looked angry and red, and Darren could feel his own anger growing. Anger at Sakura for turning his friend—his funny friend who loved comic books and superheroes—into an evil monster.

Let go of that anger, Mr. Kimura's voice said softly to him. *You'll need the light to beat Sakura. We're going to find Mack.*

What challenge will the Changers face next?

Here is a sneak peek at

THE HIDDEN WORLD OF

Changers

The Spider's Curse

Darren Smith scrolled through websites about South African tribal mythology on his laptop, trying not to worry about his friend, Makoto "Mack" Kimura. But worried thoughts kept creeping in anyway.

Up until their first day of seventh grade at Willow Cove Middle School, Mack and Darren had barely been acquaintances. They nodded to each other in the halls, sure, but they hung out with different crowds.

Then everything changed on the first day of seventh grade when Darren learned that he and Mack, along with fellow classmates Fiona Murphy and Gabriella Rivera, were members of a small and very secret group of people with magical powers—magical *shape-shifting* powers.

The four kids were part of a line of magical beings called Changers. Changers had the power to transform into creatures the human world believed were mythological. Darren and the others had learned that those mythological creatures were, in fact, very, very real.

Darren discovered that he was an *impundulu*, a fearsome bird that could shoot lightning bolts from its razor-sharp talons and create violent storms. Gabriella was a *nahual*, a powerful jaguar with yellow eyes, sleek jet-black fur, and the ability to spirit-walk in other people's minds. Fiona was the daughter of the *selkie* queen, a seal that ruled the oceans. With her *selkie* cloak Fiona could transform into a seal herself, and the *selkie* songs she learned from her mother contained potent magic. And Mack was a *kitsune*, a powerful white fox with paws that blazed with fire, just like his grandfather.

The four young Changers trained together every day at school and formed a close bond. Darren's new friends were the people who got Darren through those confusing early days when he was coming into his powers. Learning about his abilities and finding out that his parents were getting a divorce at the same time had almost been too much to bear. He couldn't tell his family about his secret powers, but his big brother, Ray, knew all about what it was like to be different. He and Darren were among just a few African American kids in Willow Cove.

I *wish* I *could tell* Ray *just how different* I *am*, Darren thought, not for the first time. He *could help me make sense out of all this.*

He would have loved to talk to Ray about his new abilities, but Darren had been warned against it. Changers once lived openly alongside humans. In fact, Changers did their best to protect humans from dark forces. But a long time ago humans came to believe that Changers wanted to destroy them. Their magic frightened them, and that fear made them act in desperate, dangerous ways. The Changers had been forced to create a hidden world. They were still devoted to protecting humans from evil, but now they did it in secret and from a distance.

The First Four, leaders of all Changer-kind, had begun training Darren and the other three Willow Cove Changers. Mack's grandfather, Akira Kimura, and his friends steered them in the discovery and control of their new powers. Dorina Therian, a werewolf, was the kids' primary coach. Yara Moreno, an *encantado*, or dolphin Changer, and Sefu Badawi, a *bultungin*, or hyena Changer, stepped in to help when they were needed. And it seemed they were very much needed, because lately, dark magic had ensured that they were constantly in touch.

Things got even more confusing when Darren and his friends learned that an ancient prophecy had foretold that *they* would become the next First Four. One day they would take over leadership of the Changer world from Mr. Kimura and the others. That also meant they had targets on their backs.

Not all of the magic community was as protective of humans as the First Four. The young Changers, or younglings as the Changer-world called them, had been forced to come together to battle and defeat a powerful warlock named Auden Ironbound. They had just accomplished that when a new dark force began to target them—an evil *kitsune* named Sakura, also known as the Shadow Fox.

The Shadow Fox was a memory eater. She could

consume whatever memories she wanted, and in doing so, she could also absorb that Changer's powers. A former student of Mr. Kimura's, she had left him to delve into dark magic and then turned on him when that went very, very wrong. She had long been underground, watching and waiting for the right moment to take her revenge.

Recently, she had come out of hiding. Sakura was determined to wage a war with those who supported the First Four—a war for control of magical and nonmagical beings. To do that, she needed followers—followers that came willingly as well as followers who were forced to do so.

Her first target was Mack. Sakura poisoned Mack's mind with dark magic. She lured him away from the group with promises of evil power. She turned his happiness and hope into anger and despair. Mack was helpless while under her control, and so, he had joined her dark forces.

It had been over a month since Mack disappeared with Sakura and a week since school let out for the summer. To avoid questions, the First Four had blocked memories of Mack from the minds of everyone in Willow Cove.

Darren understood why the First Four had to do that. They couldn't exactly tell the world that Mack had been kidnapped by an evil Changer. But erasing him from the memories of the nonmagical people who knew him still didn't feel right.

Mack isn't someone who can be erased, Darren thought. *Even if the rest of our classmates don't remember him, they have to feel the hole he left behind.* I *know* I *do.*

Mack's best friend, Joel Hastings, reinforced that belief. Every time Darren passed Joel in the hallways at school, the poor guy looked superlonely. Magic might have blocked Joel's memories of Mack, but part of him knew that something was missing. Darren could tell. That last day at school, during lunch period, Darren had tried to talk to him.

"Joel!" he'd called out as he sat down across from him in the caf.

"Huh?" Joel had said, his expression blank. "Oh—hey Darren. What's up?"

"Not much—how'd the art fair go last week?"

"Fine, but it's so weird," Joel had said with a shake of his head. "A few weeks before the deadline, I realized I only had half of the project done. I thought I was right on schedule, but it's like half of the comic I was working on just—"

"Disappeared," Darren blurted out. Joel's words hit Darren like a punch in the gut. Mack had told him about the comic book he was illustrating with Joel for the fair. It was a project Mack hadn't been able to see through to the end.

But there was no time for crying about Mack. No time for Darren to pretend he was a normal kid planning a normal summer vacation of video games, hanging out at the community pool, or meeting his buddies for lunch at the Willow Cove Café. Instead, Darren devoted all of his time to helping the First Four in their war against Sakura.

When Mack first disappeared, they searched for him nonstop. They raided Changer base after Changer base. But every time they found one, Sakura and her forces had just abandoned it. The Shadow Fox seemed to be always one step ahead of them.

The First Four suspected that she was planning to try to get her claws into Darren next. Fiona had learned the magical *selkie* Queen's Song, and that would keep her safe from any attempts at mind control, including memory eating. Gabriella had an ancient Aztec artifact, the Ring of Tezcatlipoca, which did the same thing. But Darren had no such protection, and that left him vulnerable to Sakura's magic.

So, finally, Mr. Kimura assigned another team to the hunt for Mack while the First Four focused on finding protection for Darren. Protection from Sakura's memory eating.

Darren knew finding protection was important, but at the same time the search felt like a frustrating waste of time. Each day spent hunting for a talisman for Darren was another day that wasn't devoted to finding Mack.

What if we run out of time? Darren wondered.

Every time a *kitsune* mastered a rare power or accomplished a heroic deed, he or she earned a new tail. Mack had two tails before Sakura got her claws into him. After their encounter, he gained a shadowy third tail. They guessed that Sakura was putting her new apprentice through intense training to earn a fourth. If Mack earned one more tail by dark magic, it would be impossible to reverse the hold Sakura had on him. He'd be a villain forever, just like Sakura.

We're wasting time searching for protection for me, Darren thought. *Finding Mack is more important. Maybe I should offer to go into hiding so that the others can concentrate on Mack instead of worrying about me. I'm nothing more than a burden to them right now.*

Darren was so lost in thought that he didn't hear Ray, who was home from college for the summer, knock on his bedroom door. He jumped when Ray patted him on the shoulder.

"You left your phone downstairs," Ray said, handing Darren his cell. "A Professor Zwane from Wyndemere Academy called."

Darren tried to keep his face neutral as he took the phone. "Thanks, bro."

"So now that you might be going to a fancy boarding school, are you going to make me answer all your calls?" Ray teased. "Do you need a secretary?"

Darren laughed. "If I manage to get into a fancy

boarding school, I'll probably need a tutor," he said. "But unfortunately, I'm not related to anyone smart enough. Except Mom, I guess."

Ray summoned a look of mock outrage and managed to squeak out, "Doth mine ears deceive me? You'll be lucky if I don't school you on endothermic reactions just to embarrass you in front of the boarding school girls."

"Well, now after you've said that, you're definitely *not* hired," Darren said with a grin. "Embarrassment is cause for an immediate 'you're fired.' Now let me call this guy back, or they'll change their minds about me before I even go for a tour."

"Of course, grand pooh-bah." Ray laughed and bowed before leaving the room.

As soon as he did, Darren returned Professor Zwane's call. Professor Zwane was a Changer and a teacher at the only high school in America just for Changers. If he was calling, there had to be news.

About the Author

H. K. Varian has always loved reading about ancient mythology, ruins, and magic. Though H.K. once dreamed of having awesome powers like in Changers, writing became kind of like magic in and of itself. Today, H.K. lives, writes, and has adventures in Pittsburgh, though most of them don't involve battling warlocks, storming castles, or retrieving enchanted objects.